Fate's Key

a novel by
Lee A. Morris

PublishAmerica
Baltimore

ISBN: 1-60474-565-7
PUBLISHED BY PUBLISHAMERICA, LLLP
www.publishamerica.com
Baltimore

Printed in the United States of America

Fate's Key

Chapter One

What was she doing back with Mom and Dad in Ohio she asked herself for the umpteenth time, as she gazed through her old bedroom window? For the umpteenth time, she could not find an appropriate answer.

Sighing, she stuck her head through the window. She needed to feel the suns rays on her face. She embraced the warm summer breeze blowing through her hair and took a deep breath. It momentarily made her feel energized.

Her attention turned to the lake in the distance. It was beautiful and held many memories of her youth. What did she do to deserve this? Another question, another unanswered question.

"Clare, lunch," her mother's voice interrupted her fragmented thoughts.

"I'll be right there Mother, I just have a few more things to do," she told her without moving. She was feeling sorry for herself and felt the need to wallow in her misery.

"Don't be long, your father's hungry."

"Go ahead, start without me," she didn't have much of an appetite anyway.

What had happened to her? She wasn't this way in high school.

She was happy and even happier when Chris and she started dating. They were inseparable and talked about their future together and their plans for college. They would attend the same university. Chris would study forensic medicine and she would be an interpreter and travel all over the world. It was so exciting back then. They would always be together, at least she thought they would or in retrospect, perhaps she wanted it to be that way.

"Clare," her mother's voice sounded insistent.

"Coming," she responded, trying not to sound irritated. She so wanted to be left alone.

She joined them….

"Clare, are you alright?"

"Yea, I just have a lot on my mind."

"Is there anything I can do to help?"

"I love you mom, but this time, I have to work things out myself."

"You know I love you Clare."

"Yea…I know mom and I love you to." Before sitting down to eat she pulled her sandy blonde hair into a ponytail.

Later, she walked along the lake, as she often did as a teenager to gather her thoughts. Memories of Chris and she flashed through her head. They loved to be alone here and talked for hours. She also lost her virginity there too, that was extra special. At that time, Chris was the only boy she had ever had sex with. She never really felt about anyone the way she felt about Chris. Thinking of his soft brown hair blowing in the wind and the way his tall slender body when he held her in his arms gave her a sense of completion. As she walked, she became engulfed in her feelings, almost to the point where she felt as if she was reliving the day her life changed.

She sat down and allowed the tears to stream down her face as the memories absorbed her.

The wind blew across the lake and the sun felt warm and soft on her face and arms. The smell of the spring flowers poured their pungent smell across the lake. She had felt happy, and lucky. Lucky to be sitting beside Chris—her one true love.

She looked up at him. He seemed lost in thought.

"Chris what's wrong?" she asked him gently.

"Nothing"

"You seem as if you're in a different world."

"There's nothing wrong with me," he said off-handishly.

She sat up and faced him.

"There is something wrong. Talk to me Chris."

Turning his face toward the lake.

"I don't want to hurt you Clare," he said…

"What are you trying to say to me?" With a tearful question on her face.

Turning to look at Clare's face with his eyes slightly closed.

"I don't want you to be upset."

"Chris you are acting as though you want to break up." Standing up and glancing back at the lake and then turning to face her.

The expression on his face said it all, and a feeling like none she had ever experienced surged through her body. She knew somehow that they were going their separate ways and she didn't know how to stop it.

"Clare, we'll be out of high school in a month and I think maybe it would be better for us to go to separate colleges, and maybe see what life has out there for each of us. Besides, you'll be traveling all over the world when you finish your studies, and I'm not sure where I'll go when I'm finished," he said shaking his curly brown hair from his face.

It took a second to register what he said. Then it sunk into her mind. She didn't see that coming. Tears pricked her eyes and she wiped them with the back of her hand. He handed her his hankie he always carried in his back pocket. Was that supposed to comfort her?

"I don't understand," she said trying to regain some composure. "I thought we were in each others hearts, I thought we would be together forever. What happened?" "Clare I thought so too but things change. I don't know what to say to make this easy for you but I guess there is no easy way to do this. I'm sorry."

Clare could not believe what he was telling her. It felt like a bad dream and she couldn't wake up from it. She was confused. They talked about getting an apartment after graduation. What happened?

"Why now?" she asked tearfully.

"I guess the closer we are getting to graduating the more I felt trapped in a life I don't even know if I want," he said with a remorseful voice.

"Why didn't you say something to me before, maybe I could have helped, we can't let it end like this Chris!" She said…begging.

"I thought my feelings would change, but they haven't. I'm sorry I didn't mean to hurt you," he whispered.

Standing up to face him with tears flowing down her face. "I thought maybe if we were free to explore other people."

"I trusted you with my feelings with my life. How could you do this to me? I'll never forgive you," she said angrily.

She got up and ran across the meadow. He was not going to see what he was doing to her emotionally. She paused to see if he would follow. He didn't. She ran through the house, ignoring her mother and went directly to her bedroom, and looked out the window. She had to see if he changed his mind, and would follow her to beg for her forgiveness. With tears streaming down her face, she watched as he picked up the blanket he brought, folded it and walked away. Her world ended.

"Clare what's wrong?" she barely heard her mother's concerned voice.

"Oh mom Chris doesn't want to see me anymore."

Sitting down on the bed, lifting Clare's face up.

"Clare, look at me," she said gently as she lifted her chin. "Maybe it's for the best. I mean you're going off to college soon and you will meet other people."

"How can you say that? My world has collapsed and you're telling me I'll meet other people!" She shouted...

"I didn't mean it that way, you silly girl, I mean right now concentrate on college.

Burying her head in a pillow and crying for the next hour...she sat up and wiped her face and thought to herself, there's only one month left of school.

Perhaps her mother was right. If she were busy with studies she wouldn't have time to think of Chris. She consoled herself thinking that it might actually be fun.

Chapter Two

As graduation approached things became hectic and exciting. But the empty feeling inside her was still there. Though she tried to bury her feelings for Chris, she knew if she saw him they would come rushing back. She didn't want that and planned to do her best to avoid him.

At the end of the school day, going to her locker to gather books to take home.

"Clare, she heard his familiar voice.

She turned around. Feeling her heart pumping fast as she turned to look into his hazel eyes, which were fixed on her, as her breathing began to speed up.

"Hi Chris. Congratulations.

"Clare! I just wanted…"

"Don't say it. I'm alright about everything. Let's just enjoy the afternoon and not say anything about anything," she cut him off.

"I want to explain some things to you; I don't want to leave things as they are," he said in a sorrowful voice.

"No."

It was too late for explanations. She turned and ran without looking back.

"Mom, are you ready to go? I feel like celebrating. My life is about to begin and I feel like I could take on the world," she said trying to sound chirpy…

"Okay let's go," her mother said smiling, taking her arm…

At Cibos restaurant they had the best time together remembering things Clare did as she was growing up. The anxiety just seemed to fade away and not dwelling on things to come.

The summer came and went and before she knew it, she was leaving for college.

"Clare do you have everything?" Her mother asked

No mom, but I think I have everything I need at least right now. Let's go or I'll miss my flight."

The thirty minute ride to the airport seemed to take hours. Thoughts of leaving everyone for the first time and not being with Chris and thinking if she could really do this.

"I'll get the bags, you and your mom go on ahead and get checked in," her dad told them.

"Oh Clare, I told myself that I would not cry but I can't seem to help myself, you'll be so far away," her mother hugged her, touched her head…after she checked in

"I'll be alright Mom," she said in a comforting tone.

She hoped it would ease her anxiety. She was worried about her little girl being far away from home with no one to turn to.

"I guess this is it," she said as the flight for San Francisco was announced. "I'll call when I get to the dorm. I love you mom. I love you dad," she said hugging them.

Before boarding, she turned ever so slightly and smiled. Her mother knew at that moment that her little girl had grown up right under her nose.

The flight attendant told her where her seat was and as she

tried to put her carry on bag in the overhead compartment someone bumped into her.

"Excuse me."

"I didn't mean to do that. Here let me help you," The boy who bumped into her offered.

"Thank you very much but I can do it myself."

Finally getting the carry on bag into the overhead compartment she sat down in her seat. Then he sat down.

"I'm Jeff Baines, and you are?"

"Clare Jenkins."

"Are you on your way to California?"

"Yes I am."

"Let me guess, college?"

"Yes," she answered. As if it is any of your business, she thought annoyingly.

"What college are you attending?"

"San Francisco State University."

"What are you going to study there," he asked in a queer kind of way.

He was nosey and she wished he would stop bugging her. Who was this blond hair, dark brown eyed man sitting beside and what did he do.

"You're awfully nosey about me, what about you?"

"Me…oh yea…a lawyer…and you?"

"My major will be in languages. I hope someday that I can be an interpreter and eventually work for the government, maybe in one of their embassy for an ambassador."

"That sounds really intriguing and I hope it comes true for you. I guess you'll want to eventually travel to other countries. That would be the way to go."

"You'd think that."

"You sound as though you're not sure."

"No...I'm sure, I just have a lot to think about."

"Well I wish you good luck and maybe we can get together sometime."

"I don't know about that." As her eyes glanced over across the aisle looking at some other people. It didn't seem to bother Jeff at all. But as the flight progressed they talked and talked and he wasn't annoying at all enough so that she could she herself as a friend to him. But for Jeff in the quietness of the flight, lost in his thoughts of one day of marrying her...but.

"Excuse me, Clare said to him.

"Of course, here let me get out of your way," he picked up his things so she would be free to move and his eyes followed her as she walked down the aisle to the back of the plane.

By the time they landed Jeff and she were pretty well on their way to being friends. It was unbelievable how well they clicked. But that's silly. That only happens in fairy tales. But still, Clare, get a hold of your self. If Chris and I got back together again what would he think? How can I flirt with a total stranger, what's wrong with me?

As they collected their baggage, neither one of them uttered a word. Were they on their way to becoming friends or something else?

She felt they knew that a spark existed but were afraid to say anything.

"I guess this is goodbye for now, if you ever want to talk or get together...here is my number," he said anxiously.

"Okay...I have to go now."

Clare just looked at him. He didn't n give her a chance to say goodbye, just a phone number.

She hailed a taxi.

"Were to Maim?

"University of San Francisco"

Chapter Three

The excitement built up as she neared the campus. Clare felt like a little kid on her first field trip. She couldn't believe she finally made it.

"Thanks and keep the change, she told the taxi driver as she gathered her bags and walked to the admissions office.

"Hi, I'm Gina Fletcher," redhead girl...said to her as she entered her dorm room. Let me help. What did you do, bring everything from your room?" she said laughing, sarcastically...

"You got that right. I do have a lot of stuff huh. I guess it kind of looks like that," Clare said with a snicker.

"Do you want some help unpacking? By the way what's your name?"

"Clare Jenkins, and no thank you, I can do it later."

"Where do you hail from Clare Jenkins?"

"Just plain old Ohio."

"I'm from Seattle Washington."

"Well I guess I should start to unpack it's not going to do it by itself." She tried to end the conversation on a kind note; there was something about her that was kind of annoying. She gave a little smile hoping by some miracle Gina would go away.

"Hey, after you're done, you want to go and get something to eat, and look around the campus?"

"I guess that sounds like a good idea."

She let her help her to unpack and as they talked it was as if they had always known one another. Initially Clare thought Gina quite strange but she seemed nice and thoughtful. Clare had friends back home, but they were so far away now and she would need someone here that she could talk to.

Over the following days Clare and Gina talked a lot and learned about each other. They had many things in common like coming from a small town, boyfriend trouble, that they were amazed. Or were they just pretending because of the fear of letting all information come out. The thought of telling your deepest secrets and to trust someone hoping that they won't reveal it; she guessed was a risk in any relationship.

"Clare, are you ready for class," Gina asked? Better hurry, you don't want to be late for your first day."

"You go ahead. I'll catch up with you later."

"Okay, bye."

As Clare looked in the mirror, she thought: you can do this. You can't blow it now. Pull yourself together; this is what you've dreamed of. I guess it's just butterflies, take a deep breath-okay. Finally she came out of the bathroom, pick up her books and went out the door.

Once she got there, it was intriguing and Clare couldn't get enough. As time progressed, she excelled to first in her class and then to the top in school. Everyone was proud though there was envy among some of her peers. Clare was proud too of her accomplishments. She did it for herself and herself alone.

While studying heavily for an exam one evening, Gina interrupted her.

"Clare, I heard about a new club that everyone is going to, you haven't been out very much, and gosh you haven't seen much of San Francisco since you've been here, want to join us? She asked

"I don't know. I should study for this big test on Monday."

"C'mon, it's the weekend, it's time to go out and have a little fun," Gina chided her.

"I guess," Clare said sighing.

"Great. You get ready and I'll tell the others we're going," she said as she went out the door.

Where are you? Clare heard Gina's voice no sooner did she step under the shower.

"In the shower."

"You have an hour before we're picked up," Gina told her as she cracked the door and leaned in.

"What are you doing?" she asked Gina crossly who was buried in her closet.

"Picking out something fabulous for you to wear," Gina said cheerfully…

"I would appreciate if you wouldn't go through my closet," she told her sternly.

"I'm sorry, I won't do it again," Gina said sorrowful.

"Sorry Gina I didn't mean to sound that way. It's just that I don't know if this is a good idea to go out, I don't know anyone?"

"Trust me we'll have a great time. Now let's pick out something that's going to knock everyone's socks off," she said totally over Clare snapping at her.

Since she had not seen much of San Francisco, Clare had no idea what to expect.

"Where are we going again?" she asked Gina.

"It's a surprise."

"Suppose I don't like it."

"If you don't, I'll take you back."

They drove for about forty minutes, then, there it was. The

tipped waves rushing to the shore seemed to glisten in her eyes. "I thought we were going to a club Gina?"

"We are, but I wanted to stop here first."

"It's beautiful. I never knew the ocean was so big, Clare said mesmerized.

"Of course if you ever got out of your room once in awhile you'd know what this beautiful state has to offer."

"You're right. I've missed so much," she said as tears threatened her. The overwhelming feeling from her toes to head while the warm breeze cascaded over her face.

"I hope your eyes are opened now."

"Yeah, I've been afraid to have a life other than studying."

"I wish you would tell me about your life and what you're afraid of." Gina knew that Clare was not ready to talk, but she was happy to be a good friend.

They sat down in the sand and stared at the waves rushing toward the shore for a long while. Clare broke the silence.

"You're right. Staying in my room and shutting out the world isn't good for anyone, even me," she said as she felt her throat swell to the point she thought she was going to choke.

Hiding her feelings and burying herself in schoolwork was not the answer. Gina was a good friend at least she seemed to care. She was there for her from the beginning and they had grown close.

"Did something terrible happen to you in your childhood, Gina asked softly.

No, nothing like what you are probably thinking. "I wasn't abused, if that is what you're thinking." I had a normal life. I love my parents and I don't want you thinking otherwise, okay," she told her looking right into her eyes.

Gina nodded.

"I know that I seem strange sometimes and I can see why you

think things because how I act, but the truth is that I was in love with a boy that I thought I would spend the rest of my life with. But just before we graduated he broke up with me. I guess I never really got over the experience. I mean I thought we were going to get married, and then something happened."

Clare starred out over the water as though she was dazed by the rippling in the waves, and within seconds the rippling waves became dew drops tears slowly sliding down her cheeks and to the bottom of her chin.

"I don't believe you. All this over a guy?" Gina asked astonished. "Come on Clare."

Gina's tone sounded as if she was telling her she needed to grow up and get over it. Go on with her life.

"What Chris and I had was real or at least I thought it was until that day, by a lake, he told me that we should see what life has for us out there."

She suddenly realized that she never understood what he really meant and, when he wanted to explain, she didn't give him a chance. She wondered if she had, would things have been different.

"We'd better go back inside the car; the others are going to be worried about us.

Wiping the tears from her eyes, she followed Gina back to the car and drove on to the club and parked the car in the lot. As they approached the door, it opened and she was face-to-face with Jeff.

"Hey, she said, "I thought you were going to a different city. What are you doing here?"

"My grandparents live around here and on the weekends me and a few friends come down to hang out. I'm glad I ran into you Clare. Who is your friend?"

"Oh, Gina this is Jeff. I met him on the plane."

"Hi Jeff, nice to meet you."

"And you to."

"Can I talk to you a minute? He said turning to Clare.

"I'm here with friends."

"Oh go on you two said Gina, I think we can handle being without you for awhile," Gina raised her eyebrows and smiled at Clare, then disappeared inside.

They stood staring for a moment at each other until someone came out the door and pushed them into each other.

"Excuse me," a man said…with apologizing eyes.

"I think we'd better get away from in front of the door," Clare said.

"Let's take a walk down to the beach, "Jeff suggested.

"I've already been down there and I don't want to get sand in my shoes again."

"You should have worn slip on sandals and you wouldn't have that problem," he started to laugh and reached for her hand. His touch was surprisingly gentle and her heart soared through the night sky.

He led her down to the waters edge, stopped and stared at the dark ocean.

"It's beautiful isn't it?" It was more a statement, rather than a question. Clare answered anyway.

"Yes it is, but what did you want to talk about?"

"You know, I can't believe that we met again."

"What are you really doing at this place?"

"My friends and I always hang out here every time we are in town."

With a scared look in her eyes she turned and started walking back to the club. She had to get out of this situation. No way was this going to happen or this soon. Clare felt the spark between them when they met on the plane. And this meeting was not going any further. Thoughts rushed through her head so overwhelming that she walked away.

He grabbed her arm.

"Let go of me," she said to him.

"I didn't mean to do that but you won't let me talk to you. Jeff said in a soft voice.

"Don't you ever do that to me again?"

She felt as if the gentleness that he had showed her a few minutes ago was a front to get her away from her friends to do who knows what. She ran through the sand.

"Clare stop, I'm sorry if I frightened you. I didn't mean to. Please," the tone of his voice suddenly changed.

Clare stopped dead in her tracks. She turned around and faced him. She knew or at least she thought she knew that she could never feel the same way about anyone but Chris. Yet there was a flicker in her heart for Jeff even though she hardly knew anything about him. There would never be anyone for her but Chris Iver or could he be.

Chapter Four

At classes, it was difficult for Clare to stop daydreaming. She couldn't keep her mind on her given tasks. How could she be having overwhelming thoughts of someone she hardly knew? What ever possessed her to agree to a date? "Clare are you crazy." Thinking to herself.

She and Jeff arranged to meet again at the club in a couple of weeks. Her nerves were high in her throat that swallowing was hard.

"Miss Jenkins, do you know the answer, or are you not in this class today," her professor asked.

"I'm sorry Mr. Reynolds it won't happen again," she said feebly and slightly embarrassed.

"Good, I'd hate to see you fall in your grades."

"I wouldn't let that happen, sir. You can count on it."

The remainder of her classes went about the same as the first. It was a struggle to concentrate and she couldn't wait to get back to the dorm room and lock herself in.

"Clare, are you in there? Why is the door locked? Gina asked trying to get in.

"I'm sorry. Come on in," she told her as she unlocked the door.

"What's wrong with you?"

Clare could sense the uneasiness in her voice but how could she tell her what she was feeling for a guy she just met. Especially after all she told her about Chris. What would Gina think of her? But Gina was her best friend here and she should be able to tell her anything. By not telling Gina that Chris and her slept together was so embarrassing to her, because that was that was taboo in her town. No one knew her secret. Then a knock at the door was sounded.

"Clare, why is the door locked, can you let me in?" Gina asked.

Clare slowly opened the door for Gina.

"What's wrong with you?"

"Nothing. I've had a rough day and I have a lot of studying to do.

"Talk to me Clare, tell me what's wrong," Gina softened.

With holding everything in all day and trying to hide her embarrassment she started to cry. She wiped her eyes and explained what she was feeling. "I slept with Chris and gave him all my love, I don't understand." Said Clare. "And on top of that, I'm going out with someone I hardly know."

Gina was most understanding and listened.

"Maybe you should give him a chance. Get to know him then make up your mind. Just take everything slow and don't be in any hurry. Natural things take time to cure and love is not a rushing matter."

At such a tender age of eighteen, Gina seemed to know an awful lot about life and love. They bonded deeply and told each other all of their secrets. Even some she'd never told her friends in high school. She hoped they could stay this way even after college.

Chapter Five

The weekend finally arrived and Clare was getting ready to meet Jeff at the club. Gina gave no indication of going anywhere and, further, looked depressed.

"Aren't you going out tonight?" she asked curiously.

"No I think I'll pass, I have some things I really need to get done.

"What things?" Clare asked as she finished putting on her pants.

"Just things, go on and have a good time," she said miserably.

"Come on Gina, give. What's wrong?"

"I said just things."

"I'm not leaving until you tell me. So come, spill," she insisted as she sat beside her.

Gina sighed. "It's my grades, I kind of let them slip a little and I really need to work at getting them back up, that's why I'm not going, you go on and have a great time. I promise I'll go next time," she said walking out of the door to the vending machine.

"If you're sure, I guess I'll see you later," Clare called after her and continued to get dressed.

She felt bad for Gina but she was also excited and couldn't' wait to see Jeff again. It was the longest two weeks she'd ever gone through.

The taxi pulled up in front of the club and she walked in to loud music. She couldn't see anyone she knew including Jeff, so she ordered a soda from the bar. As she sat, she felt a tap on her shoulder.

"You didn't run away this time," he said jokingly.

"Hey, I won't do that anymore, I promise."

"Where's Gina tonight, one of my friends was asking about her?"

"She had to study, but I'm sure she'll be disappointed about not meeting him."

"Guess it's just you and me then. My friends didn't actually come down this weekend which worked out anyway." "Maybe Gina can meet him next time."

"Why don't we go outside where it's quite and we can talk.

"You ok," he asked pointing at her drink.

"Aha."

He ordered a soda, and reached for her hand. She let him hold it and they walked out the door. Clare felt as if she were on a blind date.

"Can I ask you a question?" she asked him.

"Sure. Go ahead."

"Do you make it a habit to talk to complete strangers?"

"Not usually."

"Why did you talk to me?"

"I don't really know, other than just a feeling I had about you.

"You had a feeling so you started up a conversation on that basis."

"Yea, that's about it."

"You know you were cocky and you should feel pretty lucky I gave you the time of day." "I never met anyone like you."

"Somehow, I just knew you would if I pushed enough."

"That, my friend, remains to be seen."

They finished their sodas and headed down to the seashore.

"Do you live in Cleveland?"

"No, I was visiting my brother. I live in Berkley with my parents."

"Oh I see. So what are you studying?"

"Law, it runs in the family. My father is a lawyer."

Clare made a face. Just what we need in this country another lawyer, she thought.

"I guess you don't think very much of lawyers."

"Excuse me."

"I saw that look on your face; you, like so many others think that we are in it for the money. Without any feeling for the people we defend. Well I'm not that way."

"I didn't mean to imply that about you, I'm sure you're not going to be like that."

"I know where I come from and I also know my parents worth, but that's not me."

His eyes lit up as he talked about what he wanted to do with his life. He gestured with his hands as he told her about how excited he was to help people in need and not only people with money. He told her about his goals and she was astounded and impressed. He seemed to have it all laid out for someone his age and place in life. Clare enjoyed listening to him to the point where she didn't want him to stop. She too had set herself high goals, but listening to him was intriguing.

"I'm sorry, here I am going on and on about my self and not even giving you a chance to talk," he apologized after awhile.

"That's quite alright you give a very good case for what you want to do and that's something to be proud of."

"Thank you for your confidence in me, but what about you? What's your goal in life?"

"As I told you on the plane an interpreter, that's why all on the languages."

"Wow that's interesting; I never met anyone who wanted to do that, what made you pick that for a career."

"Traveling and meeting people all over the world has always intrigued me; that was a major part of my choice, and also not having the means, like you. As an interpreter, I have more of a chance to travel. But I'm not begrudging anyone for what they have."

"I've never met anyone quite like you Miss Jenkins. And I suspect I never will again.

By the time they returned to the club, it was closed. She was swept away by the sound of his voice and those deep brown eyes and, yes, his blond hair.

"I guess we should be going since everything is closed. Can I give you a ride back to the dorm?"

"I was hoping you would offer. I wasn't quite sure how I was going to get back there, except maybe walk "

"I wouldn't let a pretty girl like you walk. Come on."

"This is your car how rich are you?" I never rode in a BMW car before?" "My parents got it for me when I graduated, is there any thing wrong with that?"

"No I'm sorry if I implied anything different. I need a ride and that's all I care about."

"Come on, get in."

Clare was thrilled and excited about the ride. They drove in silence and she became concerned that perhaps she'd hurt his feelings. She did come on a little strong about the car. Or maybe he just didn't like her, she mused.

Outside the dorms, he looked at her. Clare got the feeling that he wanted to kiss her, though he didn't. Instead he continued to stare. She reached for the door.

"Why don't you and Gina come up and spend the day at my grandparent's house by the lake this Saturday? All my friends who were at the club tonight will be there."

"I would like that a lot and I'm sure Gina would too."

"Great we'll have a barbecue and go swimming, you know just have some fun."

"Okay, I'll see you Saturday."

He wrote down the directions to Lake Merced and was gone. She wondered why he didn't try to kiss her goodnight.

Gina was up when she entered the room and Clare excitedly told her about the invitation to the lake and she too became excited. They talked for about an hour about her night's events.

Clare was filled with anticipation throughout the week and when they pulled into the driveway with Gina's car they stopped the car and stared. The old white Victorian house stood tall. Though only two stories high, the sage green shutters and trellises of roses winding up the side stood proud. The porch which wrapped around it seemed to beckon to both of them.

"Clare this isn't just a house on the lake this is a mansion, Gina exclaimed.

"I wouldn't go that far Gina, it's just a big house, come on let's go up where all the cars are."

Jeff came out to greet them. His wispy blond hair was tousling in the wind. His eyes locked with Clare's and he smiled as he helped them gather their things.

I never really met his friends that night at the club, some how we never got around to it. But I guess we will meet them together.

"I hope you ladies brought a swim suit."

After the introductions to his friends he left Gina to socialize.

Gina fitted in easily and they went down to the dock for a swim.

"Come on, I want you to meet my grandparents," Jeff said to her after telling the others they would join them shortly.

"All right."

He led her through opened French doors which appeared to be a study.

They were sitting on a couch drinking a cup of coffee when the both of them looked up and saw Clare and Jeff. Books seemed to engulf the room.

Smiles came across their faces. Grandpa and his whitish slightly wavy hair and grandma the same whitish hair was rolled up into a bun. Jeff introduced her telling them how he met her. "Gramps and Gram," which is what Jeff called them, "this is the girl I told you about, Clare Jenkins."

"Oh, you must be the girl from the plane; we're very pleased to meet you." Grams said grinning from ear to ear.

"It's very nice to meet you to maim; and you to sir." As Clare extended her hand out.

They seemed to be taken with her as each one held on tightly to her hand as they shook it. Settling in as an old shoe, Clare was comfortable with them as they were with her. It seemed that they talked for hours about that plane ride and where she was from and about her family, when really it was only about half an hour, as they left the room they said her to come back again sometime.

"It was very nice meeting you both to."

Clare saw a brief smile touch the corners of Jeff's mouth, though he said nothing.

She changed into her swimming costume at the pool house and they headed to lake hand-in-hand. Jeff's friends were laughing and splashing around in the water. As they approached, they splashed them. Jeff ran and jump in the water. When he surfaced, he yelled for Clare. She jumped in the water. It was cool but felt exhilarating.

Later, Jeff's grandparents hosted a barbecue of hamburgers and hotdogs. The food was great and so was the company.

"Let's take a walk," Jeff whispered.

No one seemed to notice when they left.

"I hope you've enjoyed yourself."

"Oh I did. I can't remember when I've had so much fun." "I'm glad. I hope we can do this again sometime, Gina seems to be enjoying herself," he added.

"I'm sure she is. Gina is the kind of person that gets along with anyone."

"How about you?"

"Me? Yea."

"I guess it has been a pretty good day, with many more to come."

"I guess so if it can be here all the time."

"Someday this will be all mine.

"This will be······'·· ···· ·."

"No its set, besides my grandparents, I'm the only one who cares about this place."

"What do you mean?"

"I'm the youngest and I have spent the better part of my life here. I guess you could say it's in my blood. I love it here, I'm at peace with myself."

"I'm glad for you, it is beautiful here."

"When I'm done with college and settled down I want to raise my children here." His eyes lit up as he spoke about the place and for a moment Clare felt as if he was talking about her. But that was absurd. He hardly knew her.

"That's a nice dream Jeff and I hope that everything works out that way."

"You sound as though you don't believe in dreams."

"Some I do but the reality of it is that not everything works out as you plan it."

They made their way back to the house. As they walked, Jeff was quiet. At one point, Clare thought he was going to kiss her, but he didn't and she admitted to herself that she wanted him to. She was however, not going to be the one to initiate it. She put the thought to the back of her mind.

Before she knew it, it was time to leave. Jeff escorted them to the car, Gina walked ahead so she could say goodbye to Jeff.

"I had a great time Jeff."

"I'm glad you had a good time and hope we can do it again."

"I think I'd like that."

"You made a nice impression on everyone, even my grandparents, I thank you for that."

"It was my pleasure. Well I guess I'd better get going."

"Oh, before I forget, I won't get back here for a couple of weeks, finals and I have to study, so how about I give you a call when I get back."

"Sure that will work out fine since I have finals too."

"Great I'll call you," with that Clare stepped in the car and waved as they drove off.

Chapter Six

Clare passed her finals with flying colors. Gina, however, didn't do quite as well. Two of her subjects received C grades and she didn't seem to upset. Clare thought that if she received those grades, she would hit the ceiling.

Jeff didn't call until week after the finals and Clare shrugged it off, hoping that it wouldn't bother her. She did wonder however, why he never kissed her.

Finally he called and they arranged to meet. It thereafter became a pattern for them to meet every weekend. Clare learned and saw much of San Francisco with Jeff taking her on a new adventure each time.

Clare felt that they were growing closer but at the end of each date, he had a distant look in his eyes and pulled away after they said their good byes. Did he have someone else that he wasn't telling her about, or did his realize that she wasn't for him? The urge she felt when they were close made her mind go off in many directions. She didn't want to push anything and decided to let things ride as there were. When Jeff was ready, things could progress.

The school year passed quickly and then it was summer break.

Clare hadn't spent much time with Gina as she would have liked, but being the person she was, she understood. So when Gina asked if she would like to spend the summer with her in Seattle, she was elated. However, Clare needed to check with her parents in case they had a prearranged plans.

They were a little disappointed but understood and were ok about it. Gina was beside herself and the more they talk about it the more excited they became. Clare now had to tell Jeff she would be away for the summer.

They arranged to meet at the club and as she entered, their eyes met. He moved toward her and as they stood facing each other, someone bumped into him pushing him against her. A surge of electricity filtered through her body. Clare wanted Jeff to kiss her there and then.

"It's a little crowed huh, maybe we should sit down," he said.

"Sure," the moment was gone.

"How did finals go?"

"I was prepared; I passed all of my courses. How about you?"

"Me too."

For a moment he was quiet, and then he said: "Clare, what are your plans for the summer break?"

"Why do you want to know?"

"I thought you might consider staying at Lake Merced for the summer, with me and my grandparents."

"Jeff I hardly know them."

"But they would love to have you. I've already discussed this with them and they said it would be all right for you to stay."

"I'm sorry but I've already agreed to stay with Gina for the summer, besides I wouldn't feel comfortable staying with people I hardly knew, you do understand don't you?"

"I guess I'll have to, but I sure wish you would reconsider and spent it with me."

"I don't know what to say."

"So where does Gina live?"

"Seattle Washington."

"That's a nice place you'll have a great time there."

"I'll be back this fall. Why don't you give me a call then, and we can get together, and tell each other how our summer went."

"I guess, but I'm sure going to miss you. I should go I'm expected at my grandparents for dinner. Goodbye Clare, have fun," he got up.

"Jeff,"

He looked down at her and for a moment Clare thought he would kiss her goodbye. A slight smile touched the corners of his mouth and he raised his hand in a wave and left.

Clare blinked as she watched him go. A tear tricked down her face. What was wrong with this picture? Her thoughts were on the kiss that never happened, and probably never would. Was this all he wanted in a relationship, a friend and nothing more? She sighed.

As she drove back to the dorm, she wondered what he was thinking about as he drove to Lake Merced. Was he thinking about the same things she was or did he not even care. That was silly. Of course he cared, but not in that way she wanted him to. He thought about her as a good friend and that should be enough for her.

She was looking forward to having the time of her life with Gina. Once in the air, she took a sip of beverage and her thoughts flashed to Jeff. She pondered over their relationship during winter. I never really explained my relationship with Jeff and Gina being the good friend she was she never asked. I decided for the time being to keep this one thing to myself even though Gina and she talked about everything else. All she wanted was just to have fun without all the complications, and not have to explain anything. Besides what if things didn't work out between Jeff and her. Getting back to reality Clare glanced over at Gina and thought this was going to be an experience that she would never forget. The plane landed on time in Seattle and Gina's parents were there to meet them. She knew from the moment she met them that they were just like Gina very friendly and easy going.

That summer was the best time she'd ever had and when it was time to go back to college, she didn't want to go. She had met so many of Gina's friends and hung out with them at the beach, went to movies and even had sleep over parties. Clare's mind was so busy that she didn't have time to think about Jeff, much less anything else. As they packed for their return, she told Gina that she felt guilty about not thinking of Jeff. Not once did Gina ask her how serious she and Jeff were and where it was leading. Gina thought in Clare in her own time would open up and tell her, in which she finally did. The only part Clare left out was about him never kissing her.

Gina was glad that Clare told her and to be careful about getting involved because of her ambitions. Clare smiled and shook her head and told her not to worry. She knew exactly what she was doing.

"I know what I'm doing Gina and thanks for listening."

On the plane, Gina stared at her glass. Clare asked her if anything was wrong, but she kept on starring. A few moments later she said she was alright and not to worry. The rest of the flight was quiet as Clare respected her privacy.

"Boy, this sure was a nice flight." Clare said with an edgy voice.

When they landed, Gina grabbed her arm. Clare turned around to look at her.

"Thanks, for coming this summer." she said and smile

Clare nodded. A bunch of friends came to pick them up and

they sounded like cackling hens in a henhouse as they talked over each other making noise that made people stare.

Clare thoughts wondered off to Jeff as they drove down familiar roads. Should she call him or wait for him to call her? What should she do? She rolled her eyes. He should know that she was back, given that classes started the following day.

"What's wrong, you were awfully quiet on the rest of the ride back here," Gina asked.

"I guess I'm just a little tired. I think I'll go to bed and unpack tomorrow after classes."

"Are you sure nothing's the matter?" Gina probed.

"Yeah. I'm going to take a shower now, goodnight."

"Goodnight Clare."

The following day, Clare felt refreshed and ready for classes. Rushing around however and getting ready for classes brought back familiar tension she'd forgotten over the summer. But she got back into the swing of things with ease.

The weekend arrived and Clare could hardly wait for Saturday night to get to the club. Trying to get Gina to hurry and get ready was like getting a dog not to bark. Clare sat on the bed starring at the clock.

"Aren't you ready yet?" asked Clare.

"I guess so what's the big hurry."

"Remember we are supposed to meet the girls downstairs at six."

"It's only five thirty." Gina said.

"Oh I guess it is I'm sorry but I just want to get to the club and unwind. You understand don't you?" As Clare twiddled her fingers.

"Yeah I guess I do, let's go." Gina said.

Jumping off the bed Clare was ready to get to the door. Gina shook her head and with a slight snicker followed her.

Anne and Kate from Jeff's party at his grandparents' house was waiting for them when they arrived downstairs. They talked and giggled as they all got into her car.

Clare was the first to enter the club. She scoured the room trying to locate Jeff. She couldn't. It was crowded. Gina touched her shoulder and asked if Jeff was there.

"I don't know it's too crowded to tell."

"Have you tried to locate some of his friends?"

"I can't see any of them either."

"Well why don't you take this side and I'll take the other to see if we see anyone. We'll meet in the middle."

"Okay," Clare said. "I guess so. Thanks Gina."

Their expressions when they met on the dance floor told each girl that they had drawn a blank.

"Let's dance," Gina said grabbing hold of Clare's arm. Their other friends joined and they danced the night away.

It was hard for Clare with Jeff not being there, but with the help of her friends, they made it a little easier for her to hide her disappointment.

Eventually, Clare dismissed him from her thoughts and had a great time. The following day, they all felt the effects of their partying. Still, even with all the yawns and rubbing of eyes they were ready to do it again.

It was many weeks that she didn't hear from Jeff. Then out of the blue his grandmother called to relay a message from him. He wanted her to meet him at Lake Merced. She hesitated at first but the lump in her throat and the pounding in her heart told her to say yes.

She replaced the phone, took a deep breath and rubbed her lips together as she ran her hand across her hair and returned to the room.

She took a taxi to Lake Merced. Jeff stood starring out at the lake. She walked toward him. The closer she came the faster her heart raced. He turned.

"Hello," were the only words she seemed able to say.

Jeff watched her with his deep brown eyes without uttering a word; he placed his hand on her face, and pulled her close to him and gently touched her lips with his. Clare responded and he pulled her even closer to him.

And for that moment they were as a piece of chocolate wrapped up together and oh how she wanted this to happen for a long time and wished for it never to end. Slowly they lay on the ground, still kissing and holding on to each other. Jeff gently pulled away and looked deep into her eyes.

"I love you," he said in a soft and gentle voice.

Clare was stunned at first and then she kissed him deeply.

"Make love to me," he whispered softly.

She pulled away and stared at the water considering it.

"I'm sorry Clare. I didn't mean to push you into something you weren't ready for."

"Jeff I haven't heard from you in weeks. I didn't know if you even still cared about me and then you tell me you love me. I don't understand."

"I'm sorry about that, but things just seemed to pile up on me. I should have called. I'm sorry Clare."

"Jeff it probably wouldn't make any difference anyway. I'm just not ready for this kind of commitment, I have some things that I need to get passed. I don't mean to mess things up between us. I hope you will still see me and we can do things together.

Jeff, just because I don't want to make love to you doesn't mean I don't have the same feelings for you. In fact I have very strong feelings for you. I think we just need to go back a little because there are some things I don't understand about you."

"What are you talking about, what things," Jeff asked. "Why,

37

in all the times we've been together until now, you never wanted to touch me?"

"I don't think I owe you an answer for that question, besides I never question you about anything that seemed a little strange about you."

Seeing Jeff get annoyed over the question, Clare backed off and walked away. Jeff paused for a moment, and then pursued her. He grabbed her arm to stop her.

"Clare I didn't mean for things to turn out this way, I just wanted you to know how I felt about you. It's been a long time for me to be able to feel this way. I guess I shouldn't have pressed the subject. I'm sorry.

"I just wanted to know the answer to my question that's all."

"I know but can't we just enjoy each other right now and I promise that I will never, not call you no matter how hectic things get, alright."

"I guess I can live with that," Clare said. "I'm sorry too," she added.

Hugging each other they spent the rest of the day together until he drove her back to the campus. He kissed her goodnight.

She watched him drive away and felt deep down in her heart that things weren't settled between them, but for the moment she would let them go because she wasn't ready to answer questions about Chris.

"How did everything go? Gina asked as she walked into the room.

"We worked some things out, Clare said. She didn't feel much like going into detail.

The following morning, they were having breakfast when Jeff showed up inviting her to take a ride with him. She returned to her room to get her things.

"Don't hurt her please," Gina said to Jeff once alone with him.

"I wasn't planning to."

Gina got up and left the room.

"What's wrong," Clare asked Jeff after noticing a strange look on his face when she returned.

Brushing it off Jeff changed the subject telling her what he had planned for them for the day.

"Where are we going?"

"It's a surprise."

"Yeah, I love surprises, so where are we going again?"

"You're one of a kind Clare, That's why I love you, just buckle your seatbelt."

"Okay," she said complying.

Jeff picked up Highway One going south and they drove with huge smiles on their faces. Clare let her hair blow in the wind and admired the ocean as they drove by. After driving for a few hours, she was getting anxious and kept seeking answers to where they were going. He refused to tell her. He turned off Highway one and onto a road leading to Redwood National State Park.

"We're going to a state park?" she asked him.

"Just relax I know what I'm doing."

"I don't understand."

"I have everything under control just let me park the car and we'll be off."

"Off to where?"

A horseback ride," Jeff said.

"A horseback ride! You have got to be kidding."

"No come on or we will miss it."

They rushed to get to the horses. Jeff had a big smile his face. Soon they were going through the giant redwood trees. Clare's eyes stayed glued to them. She often heard of the trees but never imagined them so tall. The beauty of the trees towering to the sky that could live up to two thousand years could take your breath away. She turned to Jeff and smiled with contentment and pecked him on his cheek and turned to look at them so as not to miss anything that she might see.

After the horseback ride, they drove back on to Highway One and stopped off to watch the elephant seals at Ano Nuevo State Park and enjoyed a picnic lunch of mini ham sandwiches, chocolate covered strawberries and white wine to drink on the beach that Jeff prepared. After, they stared out across the ocean, listening to the waves come into shore while they waited for the sun to set.

"Thanks for a wonderful day," Clare turned and said to Jeff. She kissed him. He responded and cupped her face in his hand. Clare thought she could easily be with him, but Jeff respecting her wishes of not to push her into anything she didn't feel comfortable with pulled away.

"I guess we should be getting back it's getting kind of late." "Can't we stay and watch the sunset? Please."

"I guess so."

They sat in each other's arms and watched the sun set in silence. The drive back didn't seem to take as long because her thoughts were focused on what it might have been like if they slept together.

"I had a wonderful time Jeff thank you," she told him as he pulled into the campus car park.

"You don't have to thank me it was my pleasure."

"I know that. Don't say anything, just kiss me," his hand touched her cheek and he pulled her closer to him.

Clare pulled the covers up around her. She stared at the ceiling and pondered about them sleeping together, before finally falling asleep.

She awoke to a note from Gina saying that she would catch up with her later. She had already left for an early class. They met up at the local pizza place and sat at the back in a corner.

"Well, what had happened? Was it wonderful and worth waiting for?" Gina asked.

"I didn't sleep with him."

"Why ever not? Isn't that what you've wanted for a long time?"

"Maybe, I don't know."

"What did he think when you wouldn't?"

"Nothing he was very polite about all of it."

"Boy he must be really something."

"He is but how do I know for sure?

"What do you mean?"

"You remember Chris the boy from high school?"

"Yes I do but what does that have anything to do with this?"

"Gina you know how much I loved Chris and trusted him and you saw how that turned out."

"Clare, that was completely different."

"Is it or am I just wanting this to be different?"

"From what you've told me about Chris he was a jerk from the beginning and I don't think anyone would have made a difference to him, but Jeff he's different somehow, I don't think he's the type to hurt anyone intentionally?"

"How can you be so sure?"

"Clare you've been dating Jeff on and off for the past year and not in any of that time has he tried to sleep with you or even try to make out with you?"

"How do you know that I haven't said anything?"

"You didn't have to; it was all over your face every time you came in from being with him. There's nothing wrong with that."

"I never said there was."

"I think it's kind of sweet. The point I'm trying to make is, Jeff seems like a nice guy and you should hang onto him."

"Maybe you're right but I just don't know."

"Then do what you have been doing, just take it slow and see where it takes you."

Shaking her head in a yes motion Clare agreed that Gina may be right. They finished their pizza and headed back to the dorm to do some homework.

The rest of the week flew by as did the school year. Jeff and Clare continued to see each other almost every weekend until it was time for their second summer break.

With teary eyes, she said goodbye to Gina and Jeff as she headed home to her parents. It was the hardest thing she'd ever done, leaving Jeff at the airport.

"You're coming back in the fall aren't you?"

"Of course I am silly, I won't quit now, not when I have almost everything I want."

He kissed her and watched as she boarded the plane. It was great to see her parents after such a long time and she hugged them with enthusiasm.

They caught up with events and gossip and as soon as she arrived home, she ran up to her room. It held so many memories. Clare often wondered about Chris and how he was doing in school. She'd heard bits and pieces about him from her parents. She felt sad about the way they left things between them. One comfort was that he was also doing well at school and would graduate about the same time she did.

She spent the summer with old friends and her parents. It seemed she had made a dramatic change in how she felt about things. People commented on her looks though she couldn't see the difference but to everyone else she had grown up. Saying goodbye to her friends and family was hard. She didn't want to leave them. Being there made her realized how much she missed them.

Fastening her seatbelt on board the plane reminded her of the first time she met the callous boy who sat beside her. She shook her head and bit her lower lip as her heart raced and she realized she did love Jeff. She leaned her head against the seat and closed her eyes until the flight attendant interrupted her for beverage. Clare ordered a glass of white wine. She took a sip to calm her racing heart.

As she stepped out to hail a taxi, Jeff flashed his car lights. Clare was surprised to see him there.

"How did you know when I was arriving?"

"Gina told me, get in."

"I'm glad you're here Jeff because, I've been thinking over the summer, and I think we need to talk."

You've really changed. I can't believe that you are the same person that left over the summer. You're beautiful."

"I guess you can say I've grown up. I really missed you Jeff."

She leaned over and kissed him softly on the cheek "I love you," she told him.

Jeff looked into her eyes with delight and took her into his

"I'm ready now. I want you so much that I can hardly stand it. Let's go somewhere we can be alone." Clare said tenderly.

"I know just the place." Jeff responded.

Clare played with Jeff's hair though she didn't know where they were headed.

"Where are we going," she asked. She was in unfamiliar surroundings

"I have something to show you."

"I don't recognize this place where are we?"

Jeff stopped in front of a tall building.

We're here, come on get out."

"Good afternoon Mr. Baines." The doorman Henry said.

"Good afternoon Henry," Jeff acknowledged.

Following close behind Jeff, they walked through the door. Clare was amazed at the décor especially the spectacular fountain just before the elevator everything. They entered the elevator and got off on the eighth floor. Not speaking a word Jeff proceeded to open the door that they had arrived at. Clare's eyes roamed across the room.

"This is what I wanted to show you."

"Whose place is this Jeff?"

"It's mine."

"I know that it seems a little big, but. It comes with a great view." As Jeff walked over to the window.

"It is big, but also kind of cozy, and I love the colors." As she walked around the room.

Clare turned and looked at him, surprise shrouded her face. Jeff raised his hand and tenderly touched her arm. Clare felt the hairs stand up. Her breathing grew rapid. Jeff pulled her closer to him and lightly kissed her neck until he reached her mouth. He moved his hand across her back, and then slowly led her to the bedroom. The gentleness of his touch was without a doubt the most… Clare was unable to put words to it.

Then and there in that moment they made love. Clare was no longer afraid about anything or anyone. It was just the two of them all night long. She didn't want it to end.

A pleasant aroma filled the room as Clare woke up. She wrapped the sheet around her and followed the smell to the kitchen.

"Ah you're awake. I've made breakfast sit down," Jeff said.

"Jeff you didn't have to do this."

"I know I wanted to, I hope you're hungry."

"I'm starved actually."

They sat down at the table and ate in silence. Clare thought it strange that they made love most of the night but in the daylight she felt a little shy.

"Jeff, about last night."

"What about last night?"

"I just wanted to tell you that it was the most exciting night of my life. I love you Jeff. And I just wanted you to know that."

Getting up from the table he took her into his arms and held her tightly then let her go.

"Clare there's something I have to tell you"

He walked to the window and stared out across the city.

"What is it?"

"I just had to be sure," he said.

"Sure about what, look at me."

He turned to face her. A tear sat in the corner of his eye.

"What?"

"Clare before I met you I was in a relationship with someone that I ~~loved very dearly, someone that I think I would~~ have died for her."

"I think we've all had that kind of relationship at one time or another," Clare said.

"No you don't understand, that first time on the plane when we met, the time I annoyed you to death. I saw something in you that made me think that who I thought I was in love with, maybe wasn't true love."

"I don't understand Jeff."

"When I looked at your eyes, I saw tenderness and vulnerability. And of course the sound of your voice even though you were so irate with me. I saw through that, and I knew we would be together. And that scared me, because I gave my self to Shelly, my old girlfriend in high school, who I loved very much just up and left me without any explanation."

"I couldn't touch you because I was afraid of getting hurt again by someone I cared about and I wasn't about to let that happen."

"I would never hurt you that way, besides I'm glad we waited, it made it more special and gave us a chance to find out our feelings in our own way and time. Holding on and hugging each other seemed to be what each of them needed at the time." The feeling of lost loves was the common factor that bonded Jeff and Clare. But way back in the depths of their minds one question still haunts them both. Would they be enough for each other?

Chapter Seven

They never visited the apartment again. Clare was overwhelmed with her final year as she crammed in the last of her classes before Christmas break.

She would be spending the holidays at home. Gina too was going home and begged her to go with her. Clare declined. She had things to do there. Jeff was spending Christmas at Lake Mereeu. He told her his family always had a big gathering there every year. She found it rather odd that she had not yet met his parents.

Jeff picked her up and they headed to the airport. Before departing, she gave him his Christmas gift, and instructed him to wait until Christmas to open it. In return Jeff said hers' would be there when she got back.

Clare was filled with excitement. She had surprising news to tell her parents, news that she hadn't even told Jeff. Snow blanketed the ground and the trees and Clare was happy to be home. Her parents received her with hugs and kisses and seeing the Christmas decorations in the house added to Clare's excitement. It was so good to be home.

Later in the evening when they were settled and sat drinking hot chocolate around the fire place, Clare broke her good news to her parents.

"Mom, dad I have some news for you."

"What is it?" Asked her father.

"Well, you know I've been doing very well at school; in fact I'm at the top of my class. And with that I've been offered a job in Washington. I'll be an apprentice until I learn the ropes and then I will be working at the Canadian embassy."

"We are so excited for you honey," Said her mother.

"I have something else to tell you, I've met someone at school who is very special to me."

"You've never mentioned this before to us," said her mother.

"I know mom and I'm sorry about that but I had to be sure about him and now I am."

"What exactly are you telling us Clare?" asked her mother.

"I'm trying to tell you that I love him. We haven't talked about marriage or anything but I'm sure we will once school is over and we both settle into our careers."

"What is he going to do, if we can ask?" her father asked.

"A lawyer, he's been working with his father in his law firm."

"But honey you'll be in Washington," her mother said.

"I'm sure we can work all of that out."

With confidence Clare finished her hot chocolate, and went upstairs to bed.

The following day she stayed in and made cookies like old times. The next day, she headed to the mall for last minute presents. She was leaning over a counter looking at some jewelry when someone bumped into her. She turned and couldn't believe her eyes.

"You're home," she mumbled to Chris, slighted shaken.

"Yeah, I didn't know you were home either. How have you been?"

"I'm fine and yourself?"

"Wow it's great to see you. I've been thinking a lot about you. How is school going? Look, why don't we go have a cup of coffee and catch up on everything?" He suggested.

"I really need to get some shopping done and I should get to it."

"Come on, just a cup of coffee with me," Chris said.

"No I really can't but thanks anyway."

"How about dinner and I won't take no for an answer," he insisted.

"I guess I could, where can I meet you and what time?" "No need for that I'll pick up you at 7:00 pm at your house and dress up, no more hamburger joints."

Before Clare had time to respond, he rushed off. She felt sure he left quickly before she turned him down.

When her mother questioned her, Clare's response was not what she wanted to hear.

"It's just dinner mom that's all."

"I don't want you to set yourself up for a fall or get into something you can't handle," she said.

"Mom I think I am old enough to make my own decisions about life."

"Baby I just don't want you to get hurt."

"I won't."

Before she left the room, Clare looked over at the lake. Memories flooded her being. She took a deep breath, she was a child then, she was a grown woman now. She can handle a date with Chris.

On the dot the doorbell rang. When she came down the stairs, Chris's eyes lingered over her, just like Jeff's did. For a moment she lost herself.

"Are you ready?" He asked.

"Sure just let me get my coat."

He helped her put it on. To her surprise, he drove a corvette. It was ruby red but seeing it made her pause.

"How do you like it? I just got it before coming home. Here let me get the door for you."

"Thanks."

She got into the car and a flood of memories flashed through her mind. She wondered weather she was making a mistake. Silence filled the car. Not even the radio played.

When he stopped at the traffic lights, Chris turned to look at her. Clare felt his stare move up and down her body. She felt uncomfortable but said nothing. He broke the silence.

"Gee Clare you really have grown up. I can hardly believe it's you."

She didn't know how to respond or what he expected of her.

"So where are we going?"

"We're going to a place that I have always dreamed of taking you but could never afford to."

"Where is this place?"

"We'll be there soon then you'll know, hang in there."

We were seated in a quite little corner at the Akron to Tangiers's. The waiter poured champagne from a bottle that was already on the table.

"Here's to us. May there be more times like these in the future," Chris stated.

As they raised their glasses to toast, their eyes met and for a moment Clare was back at McDonalds sipping cokes without a care in the world. But as reality slowly set in, she lowered her eyes.

"Why did you invite me here?"

He looked startled then his eyes filled clouded as he tried to explain about the day at the lake when he broke up with her.

"I had no intention of hurting you that way. I guess I wasn't very mature back then. I hope you can find it in your heart to forgive me."

"What's there to forgive, we were both young and head strong and I guess we were both to blame for a lot of things."

"I know but I did hurt you Clare and I feel awful sorry for that."

As the evening passed they laughed and reminisced about times of old. When they left the restaurant, Chris said: "Hey, I have a great idea, let's go to the lake and sit and finish our conversation.

"Oh I don't know Chris my parents will be wondering about me."

"Don't worry you'll be with me they'll understand."

"I guess so."

After awhile, it was like old times and nothing had changed. Clare learned answers to the questions she had been carrying around. They spent every waking moment together until Christmas Eve and Clare invited him to Christmas dinner.

He stayed well passed midnight and when he was ready to leave he asked Clare to walk him to his car.

"I bought you this, I hope you like it."

'You didn't have to do this."

"I know but I wanted to, go ahead, open it."

"Chris you shouldn't have it looks so expensive."

"That doesn't matter its Christmas. Here let me put in on you.

As he took the pendent out of its box he reached his hands up and placed the pendent around her neck. After it was hooked he rested his hands on her shoulders and pulled her closer to him and touched his lips on hers.

Clare pulled away at first but then began kissing him as the memories of him clouded her mind. After awhile she thanked him for the extraordinary gift and went inside, closed the door and leaned against it.

She sighed. What had she done? She realized her feelings were as strong as ever for Chris. What about her feelings for Jeff? What was she going to say to him? She was confused. She remembered the hurt he went through before and how long it took him to trust her. She couldn't do this to him.

The light switch went on and brought her back down to earth.

"Mom what are you doing up?"

Waiting for you, what are you doing?"

"I don't really know."

"I thought this would happen if you got together with Chris."

"Mom I really don't need to hear this now, I'm going to bed."

"You can't run away from this Clare it will catch up with you."

She slept all of the day and night after Christmas. The following day Chris picked her up to drive her to the airport. Her parents had a disappointed look on their faces as they pulled away. But she had to live her life.

Chapter Eight

She asked Chris to drop her off outside the terminal. She wanted to say goodbye outside. It would be easier. He reluctantly agreed.

"Would it be alright if I called you sometime," he asked.

"I don't know maybe later when things settle down a bit. I have a lot to think about

"Well here's number if you ever need to get in touch with me," he said. They hugged and kissed and Clare entered the airport.

She didn't call Jeff to let him know when she would be arriving. Gina met her instead and during the drive back to the dorm she asked her if she had seen Jeff since she returned. Gina never heard from Jeff, but she assured Clare that he would get in touch with her. Gina was glad just to have Clare back.

Clare had trouble concentrating, but managed to get back into the swing of things during the first week. She constantly worried about what she was going say to Jeff. How could she explain her behavior to him and would he even understand.

Two weeks went by and there was no word from Jeff. Clare became worried and called his grandparents. They assured her that he knew she was back, but with school and working at his father's law firm, he was rather busy, but he would contact her.

Another week went by and the company in Washington wanted to know if she would accept the apprentice position. She wanted to take the job for the experience and it was what she'd been in school for. But she wanted to tell Jeff before she made a decision. She couldn't wait any longer, and accepted the post. She would leave the day after graduation.

It was her fourth week back at school when Jeff finally called. They arranged to meet. She waited outside and saw his black BMW coming up the road. He waved when he saw her. He kissed her and drove off to his apartment that she thought they would never return to. Clare didn't know if it was the appropriate place to go and kind of nervous since the last time they had made love, thoughts of Chris flowed through her mind as they drove to Jeff's apartment.

As soon as the door was closed behind them, he pulled her into his arms and kissed her. It felt good to be in his arms again, but who was she kissing Jeff or Chris?

"I really missed you," he said.

"I missed you too. Did you have a nice holiday?"

"It probably would have been better if you were there but, any way I still have your gift. Let me go and get it.He walked into the bedroom while talking about the holidays and working for his father. Clare wandered over to the window. She gazed at the city and thought of Chris.

He returned holding a present in his big hands, and a sparkle in his eyes. He approached her and a smile came over his face.

"Oh, by the way thanks for the briefcase, it really came in handy."

"I'm glad you liked it."

"Well then here's your present."

He handed Clare a small package. She could see anticipation in his eyes, waiting for her to open it.

"I know it will be a surprise and I still have to take the bar exam but Clare I love you and I want you to marry me."

Her eyes welled and she looked up at him.

"Jeff we have to talk I have something to tell you."

She walked back to the window and stared with a cold blank look over the city. She didn't know if she had the strength to break every trust he had in her. With the utter of one word she could change his life, but even after all of that he could be the one that held the key to her heart, or was it Chris?

He touched her shoulder. Clare turned slowly and as she looked into his deep brown eyes she felt a surge of panic rush through her veins. She attempted to speak, but the words would not come out of my mouth. Tears streamed down her cheeks and she pushed Jeff away and ran to the door and opened it. "I can't do this. I don't want to hurt you," she told him tearfully and ran for the elevator.

His hand went between the doors before they shut and he looked at her questioningly.

Why?

She pleaded with him to let her go and with the desperate look in her eyes his hand let go of the doors. She managed to make it back to the dorm and cried long into the night. Why did she have to complicate things? How could she ever explain to Jeff what she was feeling without alienating him?

Her parents flew to San Francisco for her graduation. They had a great reunion and they got to see where she lived for the last four years. They finally met Gina. She included her in most of conversations when she spoke with them. With Gina's help, she did a lot of growing up especially in the last year.

Soon the hustle and bustle of the day came to an end. That evening she took her parents out to eat and some site seeing. At no time did the subject of Chris or Jeff come up and she was relieved because she didn't feel like explaining anything to them. Clare wasn't even sure herself what happened. They spent the next morning catching up. She knew it would be awhile before she saw them again as she would be heading to Washington DC. She would miss them terribly.

She borrowed Gina's car to take them back to the airport and they said goodbye and her parents wished her luck in Washington DC. Clare took a deep sigh, rubbed her nose and wiped the tears from her cheeks.

On the drive back to the dorm, with memories of the times she spent at Lake Merced, she found herself in front of Jeff's grandparent's house.

Her eyes slowly focused on the red corvette. At first she felt panic then she turned her head slowly scoping the surroundings. What would she do if she saw him? She rotated her head toward the lake. He stood there gazing out across the water.

Clare slowly opened the car door and stepped out. As she closed the door, he turned and looked directly at her. She walked toward him. She wasn't sure what she was going to say or do, but she needed to make him understand about that day in his apartment. As she neared, he raised his arms to embrace her. Clare increased her pace, walking quickly as tears of joy streamed down her face. When they finally touched, it was like nothing had ever happened. For a moment she didn't want to let go. Her mind told her this would probably be the last time she'd be in his arms.

She tried explaining her actions, but left out some parts. She couldn't bring her self to tell him about Chris. She couldn't hurt him that way. He never once interrupted her. She wasn't sure if he understood or if he was confused.

For the longest time they held each others hands. Deep in her mind, thoughts of what she was doing created doubts about her life

"Jeff I really have to go now I borrowed Gina's car and I really must return it."

He gripped her hand a little tighter, almost afraid to let go.

"Clare," he paused for a moment. "I just want to tell you that I love you and I'll always be here for you."

She raised her eyes to meet his. They were filled with tears of love. She gently stroked his face.

"I love you Jeff, goodbye," she smiled slightly, turned and ran to the car never looking back. She drove struggling to reach her purse for a tissue. She could hardly see the road, because of the tears. She knew her life was about to change and Jeff would not be a part of it. She wondered if Chris remembered what was rekindled at Christmas.

Gina and she promised to stay in touch with each other. She dropped her at the curb of the airport and they gave each other a hug and said goodbye. Clare checked in her luggage and sat waiting to board then she heard her name being paged. The clerk phone.

"Hello," her heart raced because no one knew where she was.

"Clare," Jeff said.

"Jeff, is something wrong?"

"I was afraid that I missed your flight; I just wanted to tell you that if you ever need me you know how to get hold of me, and also to wish you luck in your new job."

"Jeff I knew this already what is really wrong?

"Nothing I just wanted to hear your voice one more time. It's silly I know, but," he said. Then there was brief silence and a click as he replaced the phone.

She knew that it was truly goodbye. Clare hung up the phone and prepared to board. She felt sad but once in the air the excitement about the adventures she was about to embark on outweighed her sad feeling and in no time they were in Washington. She reached up to the overhead compartment to retrieve her bag.

"Excuse me."

"Just one moment please," she turned and said and had to take a second look.

"Chris what are you doing here?"

"I'm down here to visit some friends and also to look at a job, but I think I'll stay in New York."

"Oh, that sounds great I'm glad things are going good for you."

"You look good Clare, but what about your job have you started it yet?"

"That is why I am on the plane. I will be working at the Canadian embassy." Clare replied with apathy.

The lack of interest in her voice made Chris quickly picked up on it.

"I'm sorry Clare I've just been so busy and that's why I haven't called since Christmas. Work has got me jumping everywhere."

"That's quite alright I understand."

"No it isn't alright, and I intend to make it up to you."

They made their way to the baggage claim area and talked without pausing. He offered to drive her into DC which she greatly accepted.

The drive started out quiet which gave her brain time to absorb all that was happening. The silence was finally broken by a smile and a friendly hand placed on her knee. She felt the same surge go through her body when Jeff grabbed her arm on the beach.

"So Chris, who will you be staying with down here?"

"Just a guy I roomed with in college."

"What about you, where are you staying?"

"I have an apartment my job provided already set up for me downtown."

"Well maybe we can get together while I'm here."

"That would be fine, but I need a couple of days to get settled in, if that will be ok."

"Well yea, of course, besides I need to see about this job first."

Thoughts were rushing through her mind. She could barley contain them with the excitement she felt. Maybe she made the right choice after all. Chris and she were always meant to be together or at least try after all they were together a long time.

When they arrived at her apartment, Chris gave her his friend's number.

She called and set a date with him after two days of settling in. She found herself in the same routine she did at Christmas, daydreaming of a life with him. Soon a high pitch sound rang in her ears. It was the door bell. Chris, she thought prompt as usual.

"Well aren't you going to ask me in?"

"Of course, come on in."

ϯ place," he said as he walked around the apartment.

Feeling the surge threw her body as she felt for him at Christmas, enough so that she wished they could stay in instead of going out. She kept the conversation light so he wouldn't see the excitement in her eyes or possibly the movement of her body pressing lightly on his.

"How did the job interview go?"

"They offered it to me, but I told them I'd like to take sometime to think about it."

"Who is this job with?"

"The FBI crime lab."

"Wow" you've got to be kidding, that's great."

"A lot depends on how things go this week," Chris said. "What do you mean?"

He moved closer to her and placed his hand on the side of her cheek, and then as his soft words came flowing from his mouth their minds became one and ended with a kiss.

Clare was thrilled that he might stay in DC because of her. To think that he would give up his life in New York just to be with her.

They left the apartment for a night on the town to see what Washington had to offer in the way of night life. Then ended back there. She opened a bottle of wine that she had been saving for quite sometime ever since she went on her own for a special occasion, and I guess this was it. As they talked through the night the conversation headed towards the past and the times they spent together. Clare remembered how it felt to make love with him that first time. Though they were older, she was frightened at the prospect of sleeping with him again.

Chris kissed her as he ran his hands up and down her body.

Let's go to the bedroom," he softly whispered.

Clare took a hold of his hand and with a slight smile led him into the bedroom. During their lovemaking, thoughts of Jeff kept popping into her head. Somehow the two were different. With Jeff the love could be felt, it was real, but with Chris it was just sex.

He spent the night. The following morning, though she had no appetite, she made him eggs and toast. She headed to shower and her thoughts wandered to the night before. Where did she stand with him? Chris joined her and they made love again. She felt more at ease with him on this occasion.

They walked the streets of DC and took in the sites the town had to offer. They talked and reminisced about the fun they had. It was like being teenagers again.

The subject of the job with the F.B. I. never came up again. Clare let it go thinking maybe he was trying to figure out where she would fit into his life. It was a big decision. She put it out of her mind and made the best of the time they spent together.

For the remainder of the week, Chris stayed with her and during the day they took in more sites, but it was the nights with him Clare looked forward to. The week however came to an end and Chris had to make a decision about the job.

He said nothing to her and she did not pressure him. He asked her not to go with him to the airport. They said their goodbyes with still no answer to her question about the job he was offered.

She barely closed the door when he yelled her name from the elevator.

"I'm taking the job. I'll be back."

With a smile on her face she hugged herself and leaned against the door and sighed.

Clare stayed in the apartment for the rest of the day preparing first her first day at work, and at no time did her relationship with Jeff creep into her mind. It was like it was in high school, nothing changed as did it. She

and the life they would have together.

She overslept, showered and dressed hastily and managed to make it on time. When she arrived, she was amazed at the beauty of the white modern and classic design with the four pillar entrance which seemed to stand proud next to the National Gallery of Art and looking forward to the responsibility she was about to embark on.

"Hi, are you Ms. Jenkins?" "Yes I am."

"Good my name is Mrs. Bismark; I'll be showing you around and helping with your training. Would you please follow me?"

As the day progressed, Clare could barely keep up and tried to absorb everything. By the end of the day she was tired and could hardly take her shoes off. She filled the tub, lit some candles, and turned on some soft music.

She lay in the tub, closed her eyes and absorbed the music. Clare didn't want to think of anything or anyone at that moment.

Within six-months, she was ready to work independently with the ambassador. Mrs. Bismarck was amazed how quickly she learned and retained everything. She had not heard from Chris during this time. She was disappointed as she thought they had something special. However, her job took up most of her time and left her with little time to think about her personal life? She loved her role as well as the people she came into contact with and speaking to them in their own language and relaying back to the ambassador. Clare was excited just thinking about getting her own office and the privileges that went with it.

Christmas was just around the corner and she didn't have any time to go home. Her parents were disappointed but they understood. Clare attended glamorous parties and met many influential people. She took it all in her stride because of her position. Though very tired at times the overwhelming satisfaction kept her going. But needed to get them shipped off. She was about to head out when Gina called to wish her a merry Christmas. They talked for about an hour. Clare realized that she really missed her. Gina told her that things were going well. She met a lawyer in San Francisco. Clare was thrilled for her and wished her luck and told her she was looking forward to a wedding invitation. She so wanted to ask her if her boyfriend knew Jeff. Gina also told her to expect a present in the mail. She also hoped she'll like it.

"I miss you a lot Gina, have a merry Christmas and a happy new year…bye." As Clare hung up the phone.

After, she mailed the packages and bought a small tree and decorations. She was invited to dinner at the ambassador's house but declined gracefully. She wanted to stay home for Christmas.

The door buzzer woke her early Christmas morning. She

looked through the peep hole before opening the door. She was warned to be careful as she lived alone. It was the delivery man. He handed her a vase of pink roses. She read the card with excitement thinking they were from Chris. They were from Jeff: "Just a note to say merry Christmas and happy New Year. I miss you and hope to see you in January around the ninth, I have a conference. I'll be staying at the Madison hotel. Ps I love you," the card read.

Her thoughts ran away with her and tears filled her eyes. She had hurt him so much but his love never died. She pondered whether she should see him. She knew she still loved him but how could she?

After the holidays, she was scheduled to leave on a trip out of the county with Ambassador Craig. She knew where they were going to Rome, Italy but not quite sure of the date.

She was later informed that they would be leaving on the ninth, the same date that Jeff would be in town. At first she was glad but on reflection she thought it would have been nice to see him.

Ambassador Craig greeted her with, "good afternoon." They got along rather well, because he was devoted to her.

He was almost like a father to her. And Clare felt that's what helped their relationship. Being about the same age as her father and the jesters of understanding, a friendship blossomed.

As they headed for the Baltimore/Washington Airport in New Jersey, they discussed sightseeing that sounded exciting and it being her first time out of the country. When they arrived at the airport they were informed that there would be a slight delay. The ambassador and his aids went to have a cocktail in the lounge.

Clare wandered around the terminal watching people hurrying to catch their flights and trying to keep up with their children. She chuckled, thinking someday that would be her. After awhile, she turned around and headed to the departure lounge. She bit her lip and a smile covered her mouth as she saw Jeff walking towards her.

They hugged and kissed.

"Clare, I never thought I would get to see you what are you doing here?"

"I'm getting ready to catch a flight to Rome."

"Oh I see. I was hoping to spend some time with you while I was here in town."

"I'm really sorry I was hoping to do the same."

"Your career is going well."

"Jeff you wouldn't believe all the things. I love my job. So how are you doing are you working with your father?"

"Yes that's why I'm here I'm representing the firm at a convention…" "Flight 942 to Rome now boarding," they were interrupted by the flight announcement.

"I'm really sorry Jeff I have to go."

"That's okay maybe another time."

As she walked away she felt him watching her.

"Clare," she stopped and turned around.

"I really miss you," Jeff said.

Clare smiled and walked away. She felt as though he wanted to tell her something but there was no time.

She was the last one to board the plane Ambassador Craig commented on her almost missing the flight.

"Is anything wrong," he asked.

"I'm fine," she said rather sharply though she knew he was genuinely concerned. He didn't say anything further. She felt confused and hurt and receiving emotions she thought were buried. And worse sounding that way to the only person who truly cared what happens to her.

The flight was long and tiresome. Thoughts of Jeff kept

creeping into her mind wondering what he wanted to tell her. Sometimes she wished she had married him when she had the chance, but she blew it because of Chris. She couldn't take back what she did.

They finally arrived and she apologized to the ambassador for her behavior. He accepted it graciously and the subject never came up again. They checked in at the embassy and went right to work; their days were filled with negotiations and the nights with fabulous parties. When she finally got some sleep, which wasn't very much, her mind was too overworked to think about her personal life. The languages she took in college paid off and everyone was quite surprised. Some of the diplomats even thought she grew up there because she spoke French and Italian but she assured them that she was raised in the United States.

They were there for two working weeks and managed to get some site seeing in. Clare fell in love with Rome and the people and could hardly wait to return.

Soon they were on the return flight and were praised for doing so well. The team succeeded in their mission to make relations better between them and the United States.

She couldn't wait to get back to her apartment to see if there were any messages. By the time the driver had her luggage out of the trunk; she rushed quickly up the stairs, opened the door and saw the light blinking on the answering machine.

"Clare it was good to see you again but I know now that we need to move on with our lives, I wish you luck in your job and hope you find happiness in whatever you do," there was a long pause, "I love you Clare. I always will and if you ever need me I'll be there Jeff."

She kind of understood where he was coming from. Still the tears rolled down her cheeks as she sat down and had a good cry.

Another six months went by with no word from either Jeff or

Chris. The time had come for her to go to New York to find some answers.

She drove straight to Chris's office. The receptionist advised her that he was at lunch around the building in a little café.

Before the receptionist could finish, Clare was out the door. She scoped the café and spotted Chris seated with a lady. It could be a co-worker she thought, until they kissed and hugged each other intimately. Clare stood staring. Her eyes fixed on them until Chris looked up and saw her. He ignored her and reverted his attention back to the lady. Clare turned and walked out. She got into the rented car and drove back to the airport.

When she arrived home there were no messages. She didn't think there would be. Jeff was right. They had to get on with their lives. She gave the key to her heart to the wrong man and now she had to live with that.

She buried herself in work, just as she had done in college. The months passed by quickly. She flew home and spent some time with her parents and friends. Even Gina flew in Washington D.C. a couple of times it took me awhile to snap back into shape because Gina became a party animal.

Ambassador Craig was very patient with her because she was very good at her job. And also he was her friend he had high hopes for her even to the point of someday taking over his job. It thrilled here that he had so much confidence in her.

She began dating but not with any commitment in mind. One particular gentleman, Dean White who worked in the office became somewhat of a good friend and a steady dating partner. They enjoyed each other's company and had fun together without any ties, hassles or explanations.

A memo advising her of another trip was on her desk when she arrived at work one day, this time to San Francisco. Thoughts of

Jeff rushed through her mind when she was interrupted by her boss.

"Good I see you got the memo, he said to her as she sat staring at it."

"Yes sir, but why me? I never go alone."

"I'm not worried. I know you can handle anything."

"Oh yea, sure, I'm glad you have a lot of confidence in me."

"I do Clare. I know your work and what you are capable of."

"I won't let you down Ambassador Craig."

"You will leave tomorrow Clare so go home and pack for about three days the car will pick you up at 10 am to take you to the airport."

Dean was in the elevator on his way up to the sixth floor as it opened on her floor she was startled to see him and jumped.

"You startled me," she told him.

"Where are you going?" He asked.

"Ambassador Craig is sending me to San Francisco tomorrow."

San Francisco.

"Ah don't worry I'm under control I'm going there to do my job."

"Well do you think I can come over tonight?"

"Of course how about seven we'll order some pizza."

"That'll be good Clare I'll see you at seven then."

Clare proceeded into the elevator and as the doors closed she rolled her eyes and let out a big sigh as Dean got off the fourth floor. The thought of going out there was overwhelming then she panicked. How will she be able to concentrate on her job knowing she's going to be in the same place where Jeff was? Clare contemplated the rest of the day what she should do.

Dean arrived seven on the dot and brought pizza with him. What was she doing with this black haired man? What she felt just wasn't the same as she felt for Chris and Jeff. They accompanied it with wine. Not once was the subject of San Francisco touched. Before they began dating, Clare told him about studying there and about Jeff, so with good reason he was slightly edgy about that city. He might have had good reasons for feeling that way but knowing Clare that was water you didn't tread around midnight. He knew not to bring up that subject in fear it would drive her away.

"Good luck with the job," he told her as he left. "I'll see you when you return."

She tossed and turned most of the night as many things and emotions were spinning through her brain. The alarm went off at eight am. She showered and dressed and at ten o'clock the buzzer went off. The ride to the airport was slow which gave her time to get papers in order. In no time at all she was aboard and being served cocktails. She leaned her head back in the seat and was soon asleep.

Once on the ground, she was back in familiar surroundings. So many times this airport was used by her, she thought. She approached the man holding a sign with her name. Ambassador Craig had a driver sent to pick her up and take her to the hotel. The driver informed her that he would be available for the duration she would be in San Francisco. The hotel suite was filled with freshly cut roses, with a note attached: "enjoy," from Ambassador Craig. She felt like a celebrity with all the royal treatment. She wondered if everyone received this treatment.

She had just enough time to shower and change before getting to work. She had meetings already scheduled.

She went down to the lobby where she found the driver waiting. He pulled the car around front. He was already aware of where her meeting would be. The people she was meeting with, she had dealt with in Rome. This was familiar ground for her.

They remembered her quite well and were pleased to see her again.

She was invited to join them at a gala dance that evening. It was an elegant affair as it was in Rome. She never dreamed such parties could be held in this city. She glanced around the room to find her party. She was highly complimented on her red sequin gown. >From her experience in Rome, Clare knew what this night would be like. She dance with each one of the Italian delegates' but after awhile slipped out one the terrace for some fresh air.

She looked out over the ocean and enjoyed the feeling of the breeze as it touched her face. She closed her eyes with contentment when she felt a tap on her shoulder. She thought perhaps it was one of the Italian clients and turned acknowledging him in Italian. It was Jeff.

"I'm sorry for that I thought you might be here Clare or I hoped you would be."

"What are you doing here?"

"My firm always gets invited to these things; I just never bothered to go to any of them until now."

"Why now?"

"I heard they were sending someone from your office. I didn't know who at the time."

"Well you look great being a lawyer must agree with you."

"I guess so it's a living."

"That doesn't sound like the Jeff I knew."

"Maybe he's changed, but enough about me how have you been Clare?"

"Life has been good to me and I love my job."

"It really seems to agree with you. Just look at you, Beautiful as ever."

"Stop it you're embarrassing me."

"Would you like to dance?"

"Sure."

He held out his hand for her to take it. He took her in his arms and gently pulled her close to his chest. They both realized the sensations felt by the two of them. Dance after dance they clung to each other until they were. The party she represented wanted to introduce her to some people that had just arrived.

"Duty calls. I have to go with these people Jeff. I don't think I'll be free the rest of the night. Thanks for the dance."

"Clare what are you doing tomorrow?"

"I have meetings in the morning then I'm free the rest of the day."

"How about I pick you up and we take a drive out to the lake for a picnic."

"That sounds wonderful; I should finish up around noon."

"Okay then I'll pick you up at your hotel. Where are you staying?"

"The Hyatt Regency."

"I'll be there about one o'clock."

Clare raised her hand to indicate she was on her way. She turned slightly back at Jeff with a smile then went on her way. She didn't see him the rest of the night.

Clare's two languages were handy in the meetings. Being fluent in French and Italian helped the business at hand. She reported her progress to Ambassador Craig. And also thanked him for the room and the limo. He told here she deserved everything for a job well done and he would see her tomorrow sometime back at the office.

As Clare hung up the phone Jeff arrived for her. She apologized for not being ready but it would only take her a moment to change. Within fifteen minuets Clare emerged and they headed to the lobby where she told the driver he could have the rest of the day off, but to be back at ten am the following morning.

As they walked outside Clare saw the black BMW. "You still have this car?"

"Of course I do, I would never get rid of it."

He opened the door and she got in. There was not one quiet moment during the ride to Lake Merced. It was like they were never apart. Even Jeff's attitude changed somehow.

When they arrived, Jeff's grandparents excused themselves, so they could have some time alone.

While spreading the blanket the wind caught hold of it and took it right out of their hands. They giggled and managed to get it down.

"I hope you're hungry."

"I must confess I'm starved."

"Good. I think I brought everything but the kitchen sink."

Clare was surprised at everything he pulled out of the basket. Right down to the wine. They gorged until they couldn't put anything more into their stomachs.

They lay on the blanket, looking up at the sky, relaxing and just enjoyed being with each other. It felt good to Clare.

Jeff turned and propped his head up.

"Do you want to take a walk around the lake? We can work off some of this food."

"Okay."

He quickly rose up and extended his hand for her to take. She took it. Hand in hand they walked on the waters edge, renewing their friendship and possibly their love. All the elements were there, just needing a little nudge. They spent the rest of the day lying around the lake laughing talking and enjoying each others company, remembering when they first met, and how long it took Jeff to kiss her, and how the longing had engulfed her mind.

Clare stopped suddenly, turned, and looked into Jeff's brown eyes, She raised her hand and softly touched his cheek, pulled his face closer and began kissing his face, slowly, gliding down to his lips with greater intent. Responding, his arms clung to her back pulling her closer and the moment lingered for what seemed to be hours.

"Is this what you want Clare?"

Pausing for moment, she raised her eyes to meet his.

"Yes!"

With that they walked up toward the house.

"No. Not here Jeff. I couldn't there, not home; besides I don't think I have the strength to wait. Please can't we go to your place?" she said with a slight grin.

Excitedly Jeff opened car door. Clare stared at him. This was right she told herself even for him or at least he acted as such.

"Are you sure?" He asked as they arrived at his apartment.

Clare got out of the car, walked to the door, turned slightly and raised her arm motioning for him to follow with her index finger. With that, Jeff got out and started kissing her at the door while trying to get the key into the lock. Embraced in each others arms they slowly moved toward the bedroom while leaving a trail of clothing along the way. The love that had been buried spun out like a volcano.

Lying in bed after, Clare decided to ask him what he wanted to tell her that day at the airport. She had a pretty good idea of what it was but she wanted him to tell her.

"Do you remember the time when you had the conference in DC and we ran into each other at the airport? Remember I was on my way to Rome and my flight was called? What were you trying to tell me?"

"I don't think we need to discuss that do we?"

"I would really like to know, it would mean a lot to me please?"

Jeff rose up from the bed, grabbed a robe and walked to the other room. Clare followed determined to get an answer. He started fixing coffee in the kitchen.

"Jeff why are you avoiding this?"

"I'm not avoiding anything."

"Then tell me why you left the bedroom in such a hurry."

"Alright I just wanted to tell you that I loved you and I know you studied hard to get where you wanted to go in your career, that I understood and I would be here if you ever needed me."

"I know you do Jeff, you've told me so many times before."

"I know; I just wanted you to know again."

"Oh Jeff! Tears streamed down her cheeks, she hugged him not ever wanting to let go.

"I love you Jeff and I'm sorry for a lot of things I've done but don't ever doubt the feelings I have for you."

They began kissing and holding each other. There was still one question in Jeff's mind however; he wasn't sure if he should bring it up, or just let it go. But it was a question that needed to be answered it their relationship was going to continue.

"Clare, now that we are clearing the air; I need to know why you turned down my marriage proposal. I never would have stopped you from pursuing your career. I know you would have done that then why Clare why?"

"I guess I wasn't ready for that kind of commitment."

"I don't think that's a very good answer."

"Jeff at this time it's the best I can offer, anyway we're together now, and lets enjoy what we have right now." "Okay."

Clare threw her arms around Jeff and hugged him. Reaching over to turn the coffee off Jeff picked her up and carried her to the bed room.

The next morning Clare awoke before Jeff, creeping into the

bathroom as quietly as she could. She took a shower, feeling the warm drops of water spraying on her body.

"Can I join you I think there's enough room for both of us?"

Jeff began caressing her body, kissing her neck while turning her around pressing his lips around her face eventually finding her mouth. Pulling their bodies together never wanting the moment to end.

Jeff drove her to the hotel and Clare invited him up but he declined. He felt he should show up at work for at least part of the day. They laughed and arranged to meet in DC that weekend. Clare was anxious to show him around town. As she opened the door to get out of the car, he grabbed he hand.

"You know Jeff there was a time when you couldn't do that, like the time at the lake."

"Clare I love you with all my heart and soul," he said.

"I know. I'll see you Friday at the airport. Just let me know what time you'll be arriving."

Clare checked the front desk for messages. There were several from the office and from Ambassador Craig. As she rode in the elevator read them. Most of them could wait until she arrived back at her office. As she opened the door to her suite, the phone began to ring. She rushed to answer it thinking it was Jeff. It was Ambassador Craig.

"Where have you been Clare? I was so worried."

"I'm just fine sir."

"Did everything work out to your mutual satisfaction?"

"What do you mean by that?"

The ambassador was toying with her and by the sound of his voice a lot of things must have been straighten out. By his tone she figured out he had something to do with everything that happened in San Francisco.

"Thank you I'm glad I came to work for you."

"No thanks needed see you when you get back here."

Clare hung up the phone and fell back on the bed wrapping her arms around herself and rolling over. She was very pleased at that moment. She caught herself, she had to pack. The limo driver was waiting. Somehow she knew he would be. He took her bags and showed her to the car. They arrived at the airport and after checking in she sat down and thought about all the things that had happened over the week. Arriving back at the office she felt confident on a job well done sand quickly resumed her daily routine. Dean showed up at her office, greeting her with a kiss on the cheek.

"So how did it go in San Francisco," he asked.

"I think it went rather well for my first time alone, but I haven't heard from the boss yet."

"I don't think you'll have any problems with that part especially since you're his pet."

"What's that suppose to mean?"

"Nothing."

"Come on spill it Dean."

"Let's face it Clare you can do no wrong around here not like the rest of us."

"I want you to leave my office now Dean."

"Come on Clare, don't take it so personally. I'm sorry but you asked. Can I still come over tonight if that's okay so we can talk about this?"

"I don't think so I still have to unpack and some others things."

"I'm sorry. Don't be mad."

"I'm not Dean I just don't want to do anything tonight okay."

"Sure I understand I'll see you later Clare."

Feeling like a scolded dog dean left her office closing the door behind him. Clare rolled her eyes, and went back to her desk, and laid her head down. Ambassador Craig knocked while easing the door open. He stepped in.

"I've come with the results of your trip. Looking at them you received an excellent rating. You've done the office proud Clare."

"Thank you sir, but you're not just saying that because of our friendship are you?"

"Clare we may be very good friends but that would never interfere with judgment calls on the job; if you messed up I'd be the first to tell you."

"I really appreciate your saying that because I wouldn't want to be known as your pet."

"Why would you say something like that? Have people been talking?"

"Some people have."

"Don't worry about what some people gossip about, anyway other than the job, what other things did you get me up did you think I set up?"

"You knew that I would go and see him. How could you?"

"But aren't you glad I did send you to San Francisco?"

"So what happened?"

"Well yes things went so well that he's flying in this weekend."

"I'm very happy for you Clare," and on that note he walked over to the door and paused, turned, waved a file said: "Nice job," and walked out.

With a big sigh Clare continued with her daily routine.

She greeted Jeff with a hug and a kiss at her apartment door.

"I couldn't wait for you to get here Jeff I've missed you."

"It hasn't been that long but I know what you mean."

"Well just don't stand there come on in"

"Nice place you have here and what's that aroma, what ever it is it smells great."

"I'm cooking dinner for you. There's a lot you don't know

about me, would you like to find out?" she asked putting her arms around his neck and looking into his eyes.

"And what would you like to show me?"

"Come on," she said grabbing his arm and leading him to the bedroom.

Getting the hint Jeff eagerly followed and began kissing her neck and rolling his hands over her body. There in the doorway they made love. They embraced for hours until a slight smell rose from the kitchen. Jumping up Clare said: "oh no dinner." She ran into the kitchen.

"It's ruined, she moaned.

"It's okay."

"I know but I wanted to surprise you."

"I'm surprised just being here with you. You don't have to cook for me, he said taking her in his arms trying to comfort her as much as he could.

"I have an idea let's order pizza."

"Oh Jeff, I love you so much."

He began cleaning up the kitchen tossing the burnt dinner in the garbage while Clare phoned for pizza. When she returned, he began snickering, looking at each other they both busted out laughing. It was the greatest evening for both of them.

The following day they went to see the sites of the city. For lunch they grabbed a simple hot dog from one of the street venders, but the evening meal was a little more elegant at the Inn at Little Washington and they ended up at her apartment sipping white wine while talking about the walk through Franklin Square and the bus ride to Arlington National Cemetery.

In the quite hours of the night while sitting on the couch, Jeff pulled out the ring he once offered her. Slowly he got down on one knee and asked her if she would marry him again. This time without hesitation, she accepted.

"Oh Jeff, yes…yes…yes!"

Thrilled, she threw her arms around him kissing, crying, and laughing all at the same time. Pledging themselves to each other meant healing finally in both of their lives.

The following morning they started making plans for their new life. Jeff was willing to quit his fathers firm and move to DC. He knew how much Clare's job meant to her. He was willing to make the sacrifice for her and give up all he had and knew just to be with her. Clare couldn't believe that anyone would do that for her.

They didn't want to wait so they started making plans to get married as soon as Jeff could clear up a few things. Her parents probably wouldn't approve but waiting any longer just seemed senseless. Jeff told her he probably would not be able to call her for about a month because of plans he had to make, but assured her he would come.

That evening they had dinner with the ambassador and his family. Clare wanted them to meet Jeff. From the time they arrived he fitted right in with everyone which surprised Clare. He was so easy going with anyone he met. The first chance she got Ambassador Craig alone she had to know what he thought of Jeff.

"Well what do you think?"

"You made a very good choice, I like him a lot."

With a big smile she kissed him on the cheek and whispered "thank you that means a lot to me."

They returned to join the guests with grins on their faces. Ambassador Craig's wife gave him that look of the right choice with one raised eyebrow, and without speaking a word their language was silently understood.

"Well I guess we should be going Jeff has an early flight to catch in the morning."

"It's been very nice having you both and we hope you come again," said Ambassador Craig.

"It was very nice meeting you Jeff." Mrs. Craig excused herself so her husband could escort them to the door.

The evening had gone very smooth and Jeff fit right in to the scheme of everything to get the approval Clare needed from Ambassador Craig.

They returned to Clare's apartment satisfied, holding each other's hand and smiling at each other. Entering the apartment Clare threw her arms around Jeff's neck and began kissing the side of his cheek.

"I'm so happy Jeff I never knew life could feel this way."

"I know exactly what you mean."

"I love you Jeff with all my heart and soul."

"I love you Clare," he said as he held her tightly to his body, his hands slowly caressing her back while placing his lips ever so lightly over her neck, working his way to the crest of her neck, and then to her waiting lips. The embrace was tense, and then he slowly lowered them to the floor.

"I do have a bed you know," said Clare.

"So, I know," he said with a smile and continued stroking her body, his burning lips covering hers. They never moved from that spot on the floor until the next morning. When they awoke and regained their bearings, they got up and realized the time. Picking up their clothes that lay beside them, they rushed into the bathroom. Jeff showered first, then Clare. Managing very well together they packed his suit case they even had time for a cup of coffee. Waiting for the taxi to arrive, Clare said: "I'm going to miss you a lot."

"I know, but it will only take a month to clean up all my pending cases, sell my car and just clean up odds and ends."

"I know that but it will be very lonely here without you." "I'm coming back Clare, I found what I wanted and I don't intend to give it up now."

Happy tears streamed down the sides of her cheeks, throwing her arms around his neck, she kissed him. He responded and they embraced, neither of them wanting to let go. They gazed into each other eyes for what seemed an eternity. Their intimate moment ended as the door buzzer rang. Clare turned and walked toward the buzzing sound. "Can I help you?" she asked through the intercom.

"Did someone order a taxi?"

"We'll be right down."

"Clare you don't have to go to the airport with me."

"I want to," she said as she walked over to close his suitcase and placed it on the floor.

"Well I guess we better go, since the taxi is waiting."

The ride to the airport was a quite one but holding each others hand seemed to be a comfort. Jeff asked Clare to stay in the taxi and not to see him off but she insisted on going with him. She wondered why that came up twice. Was he having second thoughts?

After checking his luggage in they walked to his gate giving them about ten minutes to say their goodbyes.

"Jeff, can I ask you something?"

"Sure."

"Why didn't you want me to come in are you changing you mind about us?"

"No sweetheart that isn't it at all, he said as tears filled his eyes. He held her tightly.

"I love you Clare, don't ever doubt that, I'm just going to miss you so much, that saying goodbye well it's just hard to do."

"I probably won't have time to call you until the end of the month. I have a lot of wrapping up of things in San Francisco."

"I understand you're giving up a lot to be with me. But I'll still miss you."

At that moment his flight was called to board.

"I love you Clare, I'll contact you in about a mouth."

"I love you too."

He raised his hand to her face and gave her a gentle kiss, turned and proceeded to board the plan. Pausing for a moment he turned and raised his hand and quickly moved out of sight.

Wrapping her arms around herself Clare stood there staring into space with a blank expression, then with a slight smile on her face she turned and walk outside the airport and hailed a taxi. The ride back seemed to take forever, the warmth that was inside her heart put a smile on her face. The life she had always dreamed of was about to begin.

The first two weeks of work seemed to go fairly quickly, and then Jeff surprised her with roses with a note saying just two more weeks left until we're together.

She smelled them, sighed with a smile, pulled out a vase and began arranging the flowers. Just as she finished the ambassador came in.

"Let me guess, there are from Jeff."

"How could you guess? What can I do for you today sir?"

"I need you to go to France for a couple of weeks, there seem to be some problems over there and I want you to see to it. See if it can be fixed or whatever."

"When do you want me to leave?"

"Tomorrow, my secretary will make the arrangements and get back to you today."

"Okay I'll finish up and wait for Barbra to call me."

"Call me as soon as you have check out the situation."

"I will sir," she said continuing to fiddle with the roses, and arranging them just right. Clare placed them on the side of her desk. She stared at them knowing they would die before she returned.

Lunch time rolled around and she still never heard from Dean which was odd, because he always stopped in to say hi. She felt bad about things; she hoped to talk about what happened between them. She tried calling his office but he wasn't around and she left a message. She ordered lunch in and worked as she ate. Soon after, Barbra came in with the ticket to France and the time the flight was to leave. Clare thanked her. With a smile and acknowledgement, she laid everything on her desk and quickly exited the room.

Clare continued to clean up her desk then heard a knock at her door; she raised her head to see Dean standing there.

"Dean, how are you? I left a message for you."

"I know, that's why I'm here. How have you been?"

"I've been very well but where were you?"

"I've been in New York on an assignment."

"Oh did things go well."

"Just fine but I want to know about San Francisco."

"Well it was a success."

"But what about Jeff?"

Feeling slightly uncomfortable, she was saved by the phone.

"Wait one moment I have to get this. I'm sorry Dean I have to go and see Barbra about the tickets, using the excuse to leave.

"Where are you going this time?"

"France."

"When are you leaving?"

"Tomorrow morning, I'm sorry but I have to go, we'll talk when I get back."

"Okay good luck anyway."

As Clare walked down the hall towards Barbra's office the feeling that Dean was watching her was over whelming as he stood at the door of her office. Quickly she turned the corner and felt a sigh of relief.

"What seems to be the problem, Barbra?"

"We had to move up your time of departure from nine am you have to leave at eight am instead. Will that be a problem for you?"

"No that's just fine."

"Here are your new tickets."

"What do you want me to do with the others on my desk?"

"Just put them in an envelope on your desk and I'll get them tomorrow."

"Okay thanks a lot Barbra."

"Good luck."

As Clare approached her office, the anxiety of running into Dean caused a lump in her throat. Hardly able to swallow she thought of how she would break the news to him about Jeff even though they weren't exactly a couple, she still felt bad. But it would have to wait until she got back. Maybe then it would be easier.

The end of the day came fast. Finally a light at the end of the tunnel, everything was done and caught up. After packing her briefcase for the trip she hurried to the elevator. She glanced down at Dean's office hoping he had already gone for the day. Just then he walked out as the elevator doors opened. He raised his hand and said:" "hold the doors please. With a smile and a nod she acknowledged him. Breathing heavily she stepped into the elevator and pressed the door open button. She really didn't feel like getting into the subject of Jeff though she knew eventually she had to tell him. But it just wasn't the right time or place to discuss it. She prepared herself for the inevitable. Dean stepped in and to her surprise; he didn't say a word about the subject. Clare was shocked and when the elevator reached the first floor he touched her shoulder."

"Do well on your assignment. I'll miss you but I'm sure I'll see you when you get home."

"Thanks Dean I really appreciate that I'll see you when I get back."

Clare proceeded out the front door with Dean beside her, she went right, and he left toward his car. He paused. "Hey Clare, good luck," he said with a smile and turned and walked away. What a good friend he'd been to her all this time she thought. But the key word that stuck out in her mind was friend and nothing more. Clare knew that even if she and Jeff had not reconciled there would be no romantic future for them. It would be hard for him at first but she felt he would accept it, besides they were friends first before they slept together. Putting all thoughts out of her mind she hurried home to pack. When she arrived home the voice mail was flashing. As she pressed the button and went to the refrigerator to get a glass of ice tea, she heard Jeff's short sweet message "love ya! Miss ya! Gotta go."

She leaned on the counter and played the message again and again. Jeff had become the world to her. She found her one true love. Returning to reality she went off to the bedroom to pack after a nice long hot soak in the tub. She even managed to watch some television which was rare and fell soundly asleep.

After a quick cup of coffee, she headed to the airport and arrived fifteen minutes early and had another cup of coffee. She would eat breakfast on the plane. She lay her head back and took a nap and she awoke she was halfway through her journey. She opened her briefcase, took some papers out and did some research. Some of the names on the list were familiar from previous jobs. That part would be easy at least, but the other names might prove to be difficult. She continued to study the paper work until they landed. Customs was always a real treat, especially for the diplomat status. The process was much smother than the normal. She was greeted at the embassy and briefed on the situation. Tempers got out of control but it didn't seem to be irreversible. The delegates which were a group of men that had seen eye to eye before when they met just couldn't seem to give a little so each one could sound his opinion. A French speaking woman Jeanette Zaff who would be working with advised her to go to the hotel to get some rest before the gala later that evening. She would pick her up at seven sharp.

Clare checked into her room and ordered room service and then proceeded to get ready for the gala. At seven o'clock sharp she was picked up and taken back to the embassy for the night's events.

As she entered, Juno introduced her to some of the guests. Clare then met people she knew and felt at ease talking to them and the laughter they experienced before came back. Before long other guests joined in on our conversations. Then the dancing began and went on late into the night. Surprised by her stamina, Juno sat down the rest of the evening. Clare danced and talked with everyone in the building or at least it seemed that way. Finally the night ended and she was glad. Juno dropped her off advising her that she would pick her up early the next morning. As tired as she knew she was, she would send the car early. Clare knew it was a test but she was used to late night parties and early meetings. She will have a surprise, she thought.

Clare was in and out of meetings throughout the day. There were no parties to attend and no one to entertain, which she was glad about. Clare just wanted to take a bath and get some sleep. She called Ambassador Craig and filled him in on the situation. He said he had confidence in her to work everything out and that he would see her on my return home.

"You know how to handle this Clare, I have confidence in you."

For the rest of that week the meetings went well. The progress made was amazing. Juno even enjoyed hanging around her so much so that she invited her out that Saturday evening to see some of the sites. Clare was thrilled that she finally got through to her. She seemed like a nice person underneath her hard exterior. They had a great time popping from club to club, but Clare had to prepare for a formal dinner on Sunday. Dignitaries from both embassies would be there and this would be the big test to see if all their hard work paid off.

Clare put on her finest gown but the gowns that some of the ambassador's wife's were wearing were breath taking she noticed as she arrived. Clare almost felt underdressed, but she wasn't there as a fashion expo. Taking a deep breath, she entered the embassy and looked for someone familiar. She spotted Juno in the corner talking to some of her coworkers. Clare walked toward them and the ambassador from the French embassy stepped into her path.

"I'm glad you came I hope you will sit with me, he said to her.
"That would be an honor sir."

He extended his arm and escorted her into dinner. As they sat down others began to do the same. It seemed as though everyone was waiting for him. Clare was proud at that moment to represent her country. Soon after, dinner was served, course by course. Occasionally the ambassador spoke to her in French. Clare responded in French and he chuckled. At that moment she knew that any problems they must have had passed away that night.

After dinner everyone entered the ballroom, music and dancing began and of course the first dance began with the ambassador and her. Spreading herself around the dance floor seemed to be her calling. After a few, she walked out on to the veranda to get some air. A touch on her shoulder made her turn around.

"Jeff. What are you doing here?"

"I'm here with some clients."

She smiled and put her arms around his neck and began kissing him. She never wanted to be released from his arms. She heard someone clearing their throat and turned. It was the French ambassador Pierre Swish.

"Are you alright is this man bothering you?"

"No ambassador," she said smiling, "this is my fiancé Jeff."

"It's very nice to meet you."

"It's my honor sir," Jeff replied.

"I have some people that I would like for you to meet."

"Yes I would like to meet them sir."

"Jeff I have to go but I'll talk to you later I love you." "Are you ready, the ambassador asked, extending his arm? Clare took it and they walked back through the door into the ballroom.

As the ambassador introduced Clare to people, she suddenly felt dizzy and passed out on the floor. As the crowd gathered around, Jeff saw the commotion and walked over pushing his way through. He saw the French ambassador leaning over her trying to give her room to breathe. Frantic Jeff pushed his way through to get to her. When he finally succeeded, Clare was coming to.

"What happened, I feel funny," she said as the ambassador helped her up to a sitting position.

Clare looked around, starring, and began to panic. She looked for Jeff.

"I'm here Clare, you passed out."

"Jeff please get me out of here, I'm so embarrassed."

"My dear I want you to see my personal physician, to see what is wrong."

"I will ambassador; tomorrow thank you and I do apologize."

"There's no apology necessary. Just go and take care of yourself."

She got to her feet still feeling a little shaken. She leaned on Jeff's arm as he escorted her from the room, passing through the crowd of on lookers, sympathy poured out of their voices wishing her well. Once outside, Clare began to feel better, even regaining her strength. Back at the hotel room, Jeff helped her get into bed and ordered warm milk from room service.

"I'm alright Jeff. I feel much better."

"Still I want you to rest."

"I will if you stay with me."

"Wild horses couldn't drag me away, now go to sleep."

"Please lay here beside me Jeff."

"Okay but just little while."

He sat on the bed and leaned back onto the head board while Clare placed her head on his chest. He drew his arms around her and eventually they both fell asleep.

The ringing of the phone awoke them the next morning.

"Hello Miss Jenkins. My name is Ms. Riggs, I'm ambassador Swish's secretary. I have you scheduled for an appointment to see the doctor at 10:00am this morning."

"I don't know if I really need to see a doctor."

"Miss, Ambassador Zaff insist that you see him can I confirm the appointment?"

"Yes tell him that I'll be there and thank him for me."

"I will Miss and we hope you feel better."

Turning back over to face Jeff and seeing the concern in his face, Clare chuckled.

"I guess I'm going to see the doctor, she said lying back on Jeff's chest.

"I think it's a good idea Clare, you really scared me."

"I know and I will go but…can you come with me?"

"Of course I can, I love you no matter what."

They embraced each other for a moment, then slowly got out

of bed and went to shower. When Jeff came out of the shower he was still wearing his tux from the party.

"I think I need to stop by my hotel room and make a quick change, don't you?"

Holding her hand to her mouth trying to hold back giggles she agreed whole heartily.

"I guess we'd better go to your hotel room."

"Yea, very funny. Let's go," he said opening the door. They proceeded to the elevator holding each others hands. Clare waited in the taxi while he rushed up to his hotel room. He returned a few minutes later dressed a little more casual.

The closer they got to the doctors office anxiety overwhelmed both of them. After signing in they took her back into one of the examination rooms. She didn't get a chance to tell Jeff.

They did the usual examination and also ordered a urine sample. They assured her that it was routine. The doctor asked her questions about her general health and whether had a minstrel cycle that month.

"Not as of yet," she told him. She assured him that she always used protection. Puzzled by her response he declined to wait for the test results. He excused himself and the nurse came in right after and told her to go to the waiting room, until the doctor was ready for her.

Jeff sat waiting for her and anxious for some answers he jumped up when she walked in."

Well what did he say?"

"We have to wait for the test results."

"He didn't say anything?"

"Nothing specific, just a lot of questions."

Thirty minutes later a nurse emerged.

"The doctor would like to see you Miss Jenkins,"

"Can I come too?" Jeff asked.

"It's alright with me sir but it is up to Miss. Jenkins."

"Of course you can come."

They followed the nurse down the short hallway to the doctor's office, which was more like a principal's office. Clare held Jeff's hand which she found comforting. "Well I have some good news for you. You're in excellent health and you're going to need it because you're one month pregnant. You must have become over heated at the party and that's why you passed out."

"But doctor we have always used protection, this just can't be."

"There is no mistake but you can get a second opinion when you get home, but I'm afraid the results will be the same."

"Thanks a lot, you've been very understanding, it was very nice to meet you goodbye."

Still in shock Clare walked out of the doctor's office with Jeff by her side. Once outside the doors, Clare began apologizing as tears rolled down her face.

"I'm sorry Jeff I don't know what happened. I never planned on this."

"Clare don't worry about anything. Look we are planning on getting married anyway. I wasn't counting on a family right away, but that's okay too because I love you and this baby is a part of that love. I couldn't be happier."

"Are you sure about this with everything happening about your job, and the move to Washington. How can I expect you to cope with this too?"

"I can handle this. People do it everyday and this will be a piece of cake."

He held her in his arms assuring her that everything would be alright and trying hard for her not to see the uneasiness in his eyes. Among everything that had happened, he didn't tell her why he was really in France.

He motioned for a taxi to take them back to Clare's hotel. Once safely back he decided to break the news to her.

"Clare, with everything that's been going on here I never had a chance to tell you why I'm here."

"That's right what are you doing here? And why were you at the embassy party?"

"I was going to tell you but you know with what happened. I really need to tell you but I don't know how you to tell you with out it sounding like I'm abandoning you."

"Jeff you're scaring me."

"Honey I don't mean to really, you know I love you and I'm still moving to DC. It's just not as soon as I planned."

"What do you mean? I thought it was going to be at the end of this month."

"I had every intention of doing just that. I had every client caught up and transferred to other lawyers except the one here in France."

"I still don't understand."

"Just trust me. I need a little more time then our lives can really begin. Please tell me you understand Clare."

"I guess I asked a lot from you. I'm sorry I do trust you, go ahead and take as much time as you need. Just know I'll be waiting."

"I love you so much Clare that my insides ache. I don't think I've ever felt this way about anyone," he said pulling her close to him not ever wanting to let go. But things would just have to wait.

Tears filled his eyes as he said goodbye making sure she was alright with everything and to be patient with him for a little longer. Clare would probably return state side before he would. Jeff made her promise to take it easy and he would call her when he arrived back in San Francisco. With a gentle kiss on her lips he left. He was afraid to look back because the look on her face could have changed his mind, and give up his career. But he knew her well enough to know that she would survive and give him the time he needed.

The rest of the day was difficult for Clare to concentrate on anything, but a good nights rest did her a world of good. The next day she was refreshed and ready to go. To everyone's surprise she showed up and was ready to work. Even Juno didn't expect to see her.

"We didn't expect to see you today, how are you feeling?" "I'm doing well and thank you for asking Juno."

"Did the doctor see you?"

"Yes he did and gave me a clean bill of health just got over heated but I'm fine now. What do we have for today?"

"Well its looks like a full scheduled the rest of the week, we're going to be busy, are you sure you're up to it?"

"Yes I am, but I have to make one phone call first."

"You can use the phone in my office if you want. I'll be in the office next door. Just let me know when you're finished."

"I really appreciate this Juno."

Clare walked to Juno's office and shut the door. She should have thanked ambassador Newell for all he had done and supremely apologize for all that had happened. He accepted graciously with the exception she would come to dinner at the embassy with him. After accepting the invitation she went to meet Juno.

The balance of the day was spent visiting people, agreeing terms and of course eating. It seemed like all French people did was eat and eat and eat.

On her last night in the city she went to have dinner with Ambassador Swish. The evening was a great success and when she explained everything, he congratulated her and wished her luck on her wedding. After a long evening of talking she said goodbye until the next time they would meet or if she were ever in France again. He had his driver pull around and take her back to the hotel.

Although it was late she had to finish packing. She would catch some sleep on the plane. She had to make an appearance at the embassy before leaving. Her job was a complete success and her country would be very proud of their office.

To her surprise Jeff was waiting at the departure gate for her. She rushed over to him and put her arms around his neck. She was so happy to see him. She never wanted to ever let him go again.

"I couldn't let you leave without saying goodbye, I'm sorry I couldn't spend more time with you," he said hugging her back.

"That's okay you're here now and that's all that counts even if it is only a short time."

"I can't wait to be alone with you. I miss you terribly."

"I know the feeling, come home soon."

"I love you Clare."

"I have to go they're boarding now."

"Call me when you get back to San Francisco, I love you."

She blew him a kiss and disappeared. She wondered how long he would be in France, but he would call her when he had a chance, if not she would just wait.

She slept like a baby and woke up starving. The fight attendant said she had some food left over for her seeing she'd slept through lunch.

She decided to go home before reporting in at the office. It seemed forever since she found out she was pregnant and her energy just disappeared. She didn't feel very well but wrote it off as morning sickness as she ate a piece of toast. She called the office and was immediately connected to Barbra who in turn transferred her to Ambassador Craig. She told verbally reported to him and advised him that the written one would be on his desk in the morning, but as usual he said it could wait till then. He was pleased with her work and she wasn't to report in until the following day. Clare did mention she had something further to tell him but it could wait

After a refreshing nights sleep she was full of energy and ready for work. Just as she was going out the door the phone rang. She paused for it to run into the answering machine and dropped everything when she heard Jeff's voice.

"Jeff, hang on let me turn off the machine. There that's better where are you?"

"I'm at home."

"When did you get in?"

"Yesterday morning. I could hardly wait to call you, how are you and the baby?"

"We're both fine."

"I'm glad you did call you've made my day even brighter, when are you coming?

"I have a few more days here then I'm all yours but I will be out of the office all day, I'll call you tomorrow okay I love."

"I love you too bye."

As she hung up the phone a satisfied smile came across her face, then sighing she closed the door and went to work. The day started out wonderful and in her mind it could only get better. As she put together the report for Ambassador Craig she felt a slight pain in her stomach which forced her to sit down. Not understanding what was happening she leaned her head on the desk until the pain subsided. As quickly as it came, it went away. Wiping the sweat from her brow, she took a deep breath stood back up and continued on with the report putting the incident out of her mind. She finished the file and walked down the hall to Ambassador Craig's office. Barbra was busy working at her desk. She was just as dedicated to her job as Clare was. "Good morning Miss. Jenkins."

"Good morning Barbra, here is the report ambassador Craig is waiting for. I'll be in my office if he needs me."

"Thank you," Barbra said. "I'll see that he gets this as soon as he comes in."

She saw Dean in the hallway and made a lunch date with him. He had to be told about Jeff for his sake. Getting back to her office the same pain began again but this time much stronger. Managing to make it to her chair she sat down holding her stomach, as she breathed through the pain it finally went away. Something must be wrong she thought. She immediately called the embassy doctor and made an appointment to see him before lunch. As she hung up the phone it rang. Barbra requested her presence in Ambassador Craig's office. As she acknowledged her, the pain returned but even more intense this time. "Miss. Jenkins, are you all right?

"No, help me please!"

"I'll be right there hang on."

Not even able to hang up the phone Clare doubled over with pain. Before Barbra could make it to Clare's office Dean came in.

"Clare! What's the matter?"

Just then Barbra entered and seeing the situation called for the nurse in the building. Trying to make Clare as comfortable as possible, Dean sat her in the chair holding her hand with a worried look on his face. It didn't take the nurse long and when she arrived, Dean and Barbra moved away to give her room.

"Clare, can you tell me where it hurts?"

"I'm sorry. It hurts so much. I'm pregnant."

"Have you started spotting yet?"

"I don't know. I think we should get you to the hospital you might be having a miscarriage. I'll send for the car right away," Said Barbra.

"Thank you Barbra can you call Jeff's secretary, and tell him what's happening. The number is in my rolodex."

I will, Miss. Jenkins. Don't worry."

"I'm going with you Clare," said Dean.

He carried Clare to the elevator, following behind was the nurse. When they arrived downstairs the car was already there. By this time she began bleeding and panicked. At the hospital she asked the doctor if she was losing the baby.

"I'm sorry you already have."

"This can't be happening. I'll leave you alone now and talk to you later." Sobbing heavily Clare turned over in her bed. When Dean saw the doctor come out he approached him to find out what had happened.

"How is she did she lose the baby?"

"Are you the father?"

"No but I'm a very close friend."

"I'm sorry. Yes she lost the baby but all her vitals are good."

"Can I go in and see her."

"I would probably wait until tomorrow. There should be some improvement mentally by then."

"Okay doctor, I'll be back tomorrow, thank you."

As he returned to the office his mind had many questions. He filled Barbra in on the situation. Everyone was surprised at the pregnancy and why she hadn't said anything.

The next day Dean showed up at the hospital with flowers. He knocked and slowly opened the door.

"Clare it's me Dean."

"Come on in Dean.

"How are you feeling?"

"I'm doing better than yesterday, I guess everyone was scared."

"I think that the shock of you being pregnant had everyone in a state and then this."

"I know but I really didn't have much time to tell anyone."

"But why didn't you tell me?"

"I was going to at lunch, before all this happened.

"The baby was for the man in San Francisco wasn't it?"

"Yes, I'm sorry I was going to explain everything."

"That doesn't matter now. I just want you to get better."

The phone rang.

"Excuse me for a moment I have to get this phone call."

"Hello."

"Miss. Jenkins this is Barbra."

"Oh good, were you able to get a hold of Jeff's secretary."

"Yes I gave her the message and she just got back to me. She gave him the message and he's on his way."

"Thank you Barbra and tell Ambassador Craig that I get out of here tomorrow so I will see him then."

"Very well, I will tell him and we do wish you well goodbye."

"So, he's coming. Did he even know about the baby," Dean asked.

"We found out together in France."

"Oh I see, so he was over there with you."

"No. I didn't even know he was there until just before I returned home. He was there with clients."

"So what happens now, you get married or something?"

"We're supposing to."

"Even though you lost the baby?"

"I don't like what you're insinuating Dean and I would like you to leave now."

"Clare I'm sorry, I didn't mean anything by it."

"Just go. I need to get some rest."

"Okay, but if you need anything just call."

"Thanks anyway, goodbye, she said pulling the blanket up around herself snuggly.

She let her mind wander and wished Jeff would get there soon. The day passed by without Jeff. She assumed he couldn't get a flight right away. She waited throughout the night until early into the morning until she finally fell asleep.

She was awakened for breakfast and still no sign of Jeff. Though a little worried Clare knew he would come eventually. She was released with a clean bill of health and told that she was still able to have children. That made her forget the fact that Jeff didn't up. She was greeted by well wishes as she made her way to her office, but not before running into Dean.

"What? No Jeff."

"He'll come I know he will."

"Maybe he's changed his mind."

"You're wrong," she said slamming her office door behind her.

She leaned against the wall with her head titled trying to imagine why there was no word from him. Was what Dean said possibly true that he did change his mind about marring her? In her heart she knew that he loved her but ugly thoughts kept creeping through her mind...What if this was happening the same way as Chris? Still the difference between Jeff and Chris was that Jeff really loved her, but what if that wasn't enough for him. She pushed him to make a hard decision about moving to DC knowing he wanted his grandparent's house on Lake Merced. The more she thought about the whole thing she could feel the blood rushing to her face.

The ringing of the phone temporarily distracted her from her questioning thoughts. Ambassador Craig wished to see her in his office right away. How could she tell him of the thoughts she was having. Her life felt like a soap opera.

Entering his office felt like going into the principal's office. But it shouldn't have been any surprise to her. He was sympathetic. No wonder they got along so well because she reminded him of his daughter who died of cancer alone and him not knowing until it was to late. He pointed out a few things for her to realize that Jeff was a great guy who loved her deeply. And also to think about never judging people for mistakes but also never holding on to things that might never happen, like Jeff maybe not wanting to move to D.C.

He sent her home for a few days to recuperate because another job had come up if she wanted it. Clare thanked him told him she'd see him in a couple of days. As she turned to leave, he said: "Clare I'm really glad you're alright."

As she closed the door, she put her finger in her mouth and smiled slightly. Entering the apartment she glanced at the answering machine. No message. She poured a glass of milk, sat down on the couch and started thinking of what the ambassador had said. Was she wasting her time or were there other circumstances she wasn't considering. She decided to wait to find out what would happen. She wasn't going to beg to anyone

Days turned into weeks without a word from Jeff, but Clare was determined to give him space. It almost felt like the feelings they shared weren't as strong as she thought, since he never called. She filled the emptiness with work. She even forgave Dean and the hateful things he said. They went out a few times as friends. Clare made it clear that there would be nothing more. He agreed though she felt he secretly hoped she would change her mind.

The answering machine was blinking furiously one evening when she returned home. She pressed the button and the voice that started talking about getting in touch with someone. I didn't recognize until Jeff's name came up. The number that was left I didn't know other than somewhere in San Francisco. She dialed the number then hung up and walked into the bedroom to undress. Curiosity kicked in and she found herself dialing the number again. "Hello," a strange voice answered.

I'm sorry but this number was left on my machine."

"Is this Clare?"

"Yes it is what can I do for you?"

"I don't mean to bother you, because I don't know what happened between you and Jeff, and maybe it's none of my business but I thought you might come and visit my grandson in the hospital."

"Wait a minute what are you talking about?"

"Didn't his parents call you?"

"I never met his parents?"

"I'm sorry the last time I heard anything from Jeff was through his secretary on the night I lost our baby...who am I talking to?"

"I Martha Baines, Jeff's grandmother."

"You really don't know. I apologize for sounding so Jeff was in an accident, and I thought you guys had a fight and you didn't care."

"How do you know about our lives?"

"Jeff tells us everything about his life except the night of the accident. He seemed in an awful hurry to get somewhere after he received a message from his secretary."

"Then he was coming. I thought he just stopped caring."

"No my dear he loved you with all his heart, there was no one else but you in his life."

"If he felt that way why didn't he contact me after the accident? I would have understood."

"He couldn't he's in a coma."

"What. I don't believe you how can this happen?"

"I'm sorry. I don't know what to say."

"How bad is he?"

"It's not good my dear."

"I'll be there tomorrow. What hospital is he in?"

"He's at Hartsville hospital."

"I'll see you there, goodbye."

Clare took a deep breath then went into the bedroom and started to pack. She tried to think of everything she needed. The night was not very restful but she got up at the first light of dawn. She showered, dressed and made arrangements for a flight to San Francisco. Every detail was set except for personal leave from work. That she would do in person. She told the taxi driver to wait for her. She stepped out the elevator and ran into Dean. "Woo...where you are going in such a hurry?"

"Excuse me Dean I'm on my way to see Ambassador Craig."

"Slow down a minute tell me what's going wrong."

I have to go to San Francisco for a while."

Stopping in amazement Dean shook his head watching Clare go up the hallway.

"You're going to see him aren't you?" He yelled after her.

Pausing for a moment and turning her head slightly, she said: "yes I am," and walked away out of Dean's sight. "Good morning Barbra, is Ambassador Craig in?"

"Yes, but you can't go in right now."

Not thinking of her actions Clare barged right into his office. She stopped and looked around at the meeting in progress. Embarrassment surrounded her entire body. She was unable to move. Ambassador Craig spoke up.

"Miss. Jenkins, would you wait outside for me?"

"I'm very sorry gentlemen please excuse my behavior."

Slowly turning and then quickly exciting the room, Clare looked over at Barbra.

"I tried to tell you not to go in."

"I'm very sorry Barbra. I don't know what I was thinking."

With the sound of a shutting door, both of them turned to see Ambassador Craig's. His face did not have a pleasant look on it.

I'm really sorry about this. I wasn't thinking."

"I do hope you have an explanation for this behavior."

"I do sir. It's Jeff. I know why he didn't come that day, he was in a serious accident and no one called me. I hope to go to him."

"I understand but that doesn't excuse your behavior."

"I know that and it won't happen again, can I have the time off?"

With half grin on his face he agreed to let her go as long as he got updates. Clare apologized again for interrupting his meeting. With that he returned to his meeting and she started for the elevator passing Dean. He had a smug look on his.

"You're going to get hurt again and I won't be here this time to pick up the pieces," he said.

She stepped into the elevator. During the ride to the airport Clare wondered what sort of life they would have if Jeff regained consciousness. Could she take care of him? Did he even know she lost their baby? They were questions she needed answers to.

Arriving at the airport she checked in. As she took her seat anxiety set in. She wondered exactly what she would see and if she could handle it. She turned down breakfast, fell asleep and dreamt about when she and Jeff first met. He had jabbered and jabbered throughout the journey to the point where she thought she wouldn't make it to college without going crazy. Then on the beach, he scared her when he grabbed her arm. Then they eventually turned into good friends and of course that first kiss she longed for. The topper was of course when they made love the first time which the way they started out, she never thought they would even become friends.

She drove straight to the hospital, parked the rental sat for awhile taking deep breaths then walked inside looking for the front desk. A little grey haired lady called out her name. As Clare walked towards her, memories of the house on Lake Merced flooded into my mind, and all the fun of getting to know one another. She knew then why Jeff loved his grandparents so much, because they knew every aspect of their lives. With a big hug from her tears rolled down her cheeks. Jeff's grandmother held tight.

"I'm glad you're here Clare Jeff will be too."

"Is he awake?"

"No but I know in my heart as soon as he hears your voice he'll get better."

"So there's no change. Can I see him?"

"Sure, I'll take you up but I must tell you something first. Jeff's father and mother didn't want you to be called." "Why?"

"I never did anything to them."

"I don't know how to explain it without sounding as if grandpa and I feel that way too."

"I think I know what you're trying to say. They don't want him to have anything to do with me."

"Well not exactly that I guess you're alright to socialize with but when he announced his plans to marry you, I think that's when they hit the roof."

"Am I not good enough for their son?"

"In their eyes no, I'm sorry."

"That's alright I wasn't marrying them."

"Father and I knew how much he loved you."

"And how did they feel about the grandchild I lost?"

"What…what are you talking about, what baby?"

"I was pregnant with Jeff's baby. He didn't tell you?

"He was been so busy with work; trying to cleanup everything for the move it must have slipped his mind."

"I didn't mean to spring that on you like that, please forgive me."

LEE A. MORRIS

"That's where he was rushing off to that night, you were losing
the baby," she said turning away from Clare, rubbing her
forehead and starring into space.

She laid a gentle hand Clare's then put her arms around her
and held her tight. It was a great loss for all of them, but Jeff's
condition had to take precedence over everything else.

"Can I go in and see him now?"

"Come on I'll take you up."

Arm in arm they walked to the elevator, got off at the seventh
floor and headed down the end of the hallway to room number
754. As they walked, Jeff's grandmother filled her in on what to
expect.

"Clare just remember that it is still Jeff."

At the door she stopped: "can I go in by myself please?"

"Sure I'll wait out here. If you need me I'll be right outside."

Taking a deep breath Clare opened the door. As it shut behind
her she was overwhelmed by all of the machines. Then she
focused on a nurse by his bed doing something with one of the
machines. When she finished she came over to Clare.

"I don't believe you've been here before, are you part of the
family."

"Not directly, we were supposed to get married."

"If I may ask, why did it take you so long to come and visit?"

"I just found out."

"I'm sorry it's really none of my business, by the way my name
is Renée. I've been taking care of Jeff since he's been here."

"I'm Clare, nice to meet you."

"Are there any questions?"

"I don't know where to begin."

"Well why don't I give you a run down from the beginning?
Let's see, he's been here a little over two months, when he was
first brought in he was conscious but he had severe head

trauma. After surgery he slipped into a coma and hasn't come out of it."

"What caused the accident?"

"The report said that a drunk driver hit him head on. I have no further details other than that."

"Will he ever come out of it?"

"Right now there's still hope. He's responded to certain things, but I think you should touch and talks to him, miracles do happen."

Clare moved closer to the bed. He looked peaceful lying there. Sitting on the stool beside him she placed her hand on his cheek and whispered: "I love you, it's me Jeff. I'm so sorry about not getting here sooner. I hope you forgive me. There's so much I have to tell you, please wake up. I lost our baby and I feel really bad about that. I need you please," she told him as tears streamed down her face.

A tear slid down Jeff's cheek. Wiping her eyes to see more clearly, she gazed at him.

"I know you're still in there, please Jeff just wake up."

He did not respond and she gently wiped the single tear away, sat and held his hand. It was enough for the moment.

She spent the rest of that day and night with him. In the morning the nurse came in to check his vitals and found Clare leaned over the bed with her head beside his.

"Excuse me Miss, I need to check him. I'm sorry, have you been here all night?"

"Yes I guess I have."

"Why don't you go to the cafeteria on the second floor and get something to eat."

"I'm going to leave anyway, but I'll be back, she said getting up. She discovered that Jeff's hand had a hold of hers.

"I don't think since he's been here, I've ever seen that kind of response from him, maybe you're good for him."

"Does this mean he's going to wake up?"

"No I don't think so, there're other signs we look for, but this isn't one of them, I'm sorry."

"Will the doctor be seeing him at all today?"

"He should be in this afternoon. The family will be making a decision to move him."

"What do you mean, move him?"

"We can't do any more for him here so he'll probably go to some rest home."

She stroked his hair, touched his cheek and walked out the door.

The first thing she needed to do was find a hotel then get cleaned up. Once done, she decided to drive out to Lake Merced. She needed to know what was going to happen to Jeff. On route she called the office for any messages. Then spoke to Ambassador Craig. She filled him in on the situation and he reminded her of her job. There was no hurry right now but eventually she would have to return. She agreed to everything he told her.

She pulled up to the house and walked down to the lake. For a long time she stood staring into the water. It was perfect and comforting. In the back of her mind she thought she heard someone calling my name. She turned, it was Jeff's grandmother.

"I'm glad to see you again my dear. How was your first visit with Jeff?"

"He had a hold of my hand when I woke up beside him. I think he truly knew I was there."

"What did the nurse say?"

"That she had never seen him do that before."

"Well, that sounds encouraging, come on in you look like you haven't eaten at all."

"Thank you. I really haven't had time."

"Come sit down and have a cup of tea."

"I think I will."

"Cook will bring you something to eat, is there anything special that you would like."

"Anything would be fine."

"Are you going to the hospital this afternoon for the meeting?"

"That's what I wanted to talk to you about."

"Why are they going to move him?"

"Because, there's nothing more the hospital can do. We knew sooner or later it would come to this."

"But a rest home?"

"No decision has been made about that. I want him to come here and recuperate."

"That sounds like a great idea, Jeff always loved it here." "But I'm afraid that it's not our decision to make."

"Who is deciding all of it?"

"Jeff's parents."

"Why don't you come with us this afternoon and we'll find out together, but first thing's first, eat."

With so many things happening lunch seemed trivial, but she had to keep her strength up. About an hour or so went by and they left for the meeting at the hospital for.

Jeff's grand parents invited her to ride with them but she preferred to drive herself. When they arrived, Jeff's parents nor the doctor were not there yet. Clare went to see Jeff while his grandparents waited for them.

She noticed his color seemed better as she stroked his hair lightly. She always loved the feel and the way it laid. She leaned over him and whispered: "Jeff it's me again, its Clare, I know you can hear me please wake up." At that moment a nurse came in and started her routine check up.

"Nurse, what is she doing in there with my son?"

"I'm sorry Mrs. Baines she said she was going to marry him. So I thought it would be okay."

"It isn't okay and I would like her to leave."

"It's alright I'll leave, but can I at least say goodbye to him?"

The tall dark haired lady glared at every move Clare made.

"By the way Mrs. Baines, I'm Clare Jenkins, the girl Jeff was about to marry."

The dark haired lady, Mrs. Baines rolled her eyes at Clare.

"Just make it fast and don't come around again."

Turning back to Jeff, she held his hand. "Jeff I have to go, I don't want to cause any problems with your family. I hope you get better because I love you and I'll be waiting for you," she said wiping away the tears from her cheeks with her free hand. She glanced at him for the last time. Suddenly his eyes opened.

Excited by this Clare thought he was waking up, but it was just a muscle reaction. Breathing a sigh and slightly wetting he lips, Clare knew someday he would come back to her. Kissing him on the forehead and saying goodbye.

With that she walked out of the room passing everyone. Jeff's grandmother followed behind apologizing for her daughter's behavior. Taking it all in stride Clare understood how they felt, they never really new her and this wasn't the time for any of that especially under the circumstances. Jeff's grandmother tried to explain some of her feelings towards her and what she based them on because of trying to rope Jeff by getting pregnant. She was only trying to protect her son from anymore hurt.

No one new of the baby she'd lost and for the time being she suggested Clare did not to mention it. Clare agreed with her. Besides it probably would be for the best, if she left for now. Clare would return to her job and grandma promised to keep her informed of his progress. Shortly after their conversation Clare walked to the elevator. Before the doors opened the nurse tapped her on her shoulder.

"I'm very sorry for what happened back there," she apologized to Clare.

"It's not your fault but I did want to tell someone, just before I left Jeff opened his eyes."

"I'm afraid all comatose patients do that. Jeff is no different."

"No you don't understand, I mean he looked right at me, following me with his eyes."

"Why didn't you tell me, I would have gotten the doctor?"

"I think that was just Jeff and my moment together to say our goodbyes and that's enough for me right now."

"I will inform the doctor what has happened he will want to check it out. Oh, and one other thing I overheard you're leaving his mother and grandmother if you want to see him come back after 10 O'clock, the family won't be around after that."

"Maybe I will thank you."

The doors to the elevator opened and Clare step inside, she turned and smiled at the nurse. During the drive back to the hotel she was full of thought. A lot of things had happened. What did the future hold for all the people that surrounded her life? She arriving at the hotel feeling like the world just tumbled down around her. She paced around the room trying to kill time not wanting to pack her suitcase. Thoughts continued stirring around her mind. She called the office and advised Barbra that she would be back the following day around noon. As she hung up the phone, tears streamed down her face. The previous month's events that she had built up took its toll and she finally broke down and cried profusely. The release was long in coming.

She lay on the bed and was soon asleep until she was awoken suddenly by a thought. When she looked at her watch it was eleven o'clock that night. Stretching and yawning she sat up in the bed, taking a moment she got up and went to the bathroom to freshen up. Once dressed in clean clothes, she headed back to the hospital. Just as the nurse had said it was all quite in Jeff's room. Quietly she went in and sat beside him. Taking a hold of his hand and leaning over kissing him on the fore head, then whispering, "Jeff it's me Clare; please open your eyes."

There was no movement in them. But Clare knew he heard her. She kept talking to him throughout the night hoping for some kind of response. Early the following morning sleeping with her head beside his, a gentle touch on the shoulder woke her up.

"I'm sorry Miss you'll have to step outside, I need to check him."

"That's okay I'm leaving anyway, but can I just have a minute please?"

"I'll be outside the door."

"Jeff, wake up," she whispered.

He opened his eyes responding to her voice.

"I have to leave now, I won't be coming back for awhile, and maybe you'll come and see me in DC. I would be glad to have you."

Tears filled her eyes as she spoke to him. Then slowly his eyes closed and a single tear slid down his face. It almost seemed that he knew what was happening. She placed a kiss on the forehead, rose up and turned around to discover the doctor standing right behind her.

"I've never seen him respond in that way. That's very encouraging."

"So do you think he will come out of it soon?"

"There's no way of predicting coma patients, I'm sorry."

"Well I guess I'd better be going."

Excusing herself she left the room and drove back to the hotel.

She took a quick shower, changed her clothes, checked out and flew back to DC.

She left the most important part of her life behind and she had no clue of what would happen. The only thing she knew was her job. She didn't stay in her apartment long. It felt empty and very lonely.

Walking to work was refreshing and gave her a chance to clear her head. Washington DC was a beautiful city if people just took the time and really saw it.

She went straight to work. She was amazed at the pile of files that built up over a few days. A knock at the door interrupted her and she raised her head.

"You're back, is everything okay?"

"Not now Dean I'm busy."

"Okay, if you need to talk I'm here."

The fiery look in her eyes told him to back off, that it was not the time to pursue anything. Soon after he left the phone rang.

"Hello, Miss Jenkins, this is Barbra, Ambassador Craig would like to see you in his office."

"I'll be right there."

Hanging up the phone she walked down the hall to his office.

"Hello Barbara."

"Welcome back Miss Jenkins, go right in he's expecting you."

"Thank you."

She knocked on the door and went in shutting it behind her. Ambassador Craig always took an interest in Clare's life. Maybe because she reminded him so much of his own daughter that died. Their friendship ran as deep with her own mother and father. Although she'd hadn't gone home in a long time. She explained everything to him and it seemed to make her feel better. She remembered what he told me about never judging people for mistakes and holding on to things that will never be. How could he have had so much insight on things? It was amazing. They ended their talk and she went back to her office and continuously worked.

Over the next few months, the news never changed about Jeff aside from moving him to a recovering home. Maybe that was best for him at least he would be away from his mother. Trips for her job came and went with her receiving excellent ratings on all of them, but yet there was still something missing in her life.

That Christmas she went home. It had been along time since she and her parents were together and they had a lot of catching up to do. She didn't bring up the subject of Jeff. She felt it was best for the time being not to say anything. Despite everything she had a wonderful time. She stayed until after new years and it was, as usual, sad when it was time to leave though she was ready to return to work.

She listened to her messages as she poured a soda. The last three caught her attention. Dean wanted her to forgive him for being such a jerk; Jeff's grandma said Jeff seemed to be improving a bit and Gina was going to be in town for a couple of days and wanted to get together. She would call at the end of the week when she arrived.

Saturday morning came with a bright and early call from Gina. Clare sat up in bed and screamed with delight. She asked where she was she told her that she was at the Lax Hotel and that she had brought along a companion, some how that didn't surprise Clare. They agreed to meet at the Washington monument at one o'clock.

"I can't wait to see you Gina."

"Me to Clare."

Before she hung up the phone she could hear a mans voice in the background, then got up to take a shower. Putting on a pair of jeans, because knowing Gina you didn't really know where you party time! Grinning from ear to ear anticipating the reunion between them.

Right on the button she was at the monument when she heard her name being yelled, she turned, saw Gina began to run towards her.

"Gina its great to see you, I've really missed you; you have not changed a bit."

"Clare you're just as pretty as you were in college."

"So how have you been?"

"I've been doing very well, but there is someone I would like you to meet."

"And who is this unlucky redheaded fellow?"

"Ha, ha Clare this is Charlie Long."

"It's very nice to meet you Charlie."

"I think I would probably know you anywhere, Gina talks about you so much."

"Hey you two! Like do you know I'm even here?"

"What do you say Charlie should we just leave her here and get something to eat?"

"Very funny Clare! Let's go."

They spent the remainder of the day sight seeing and late that evening they went to dinner and dancing.

Clare kept trying to get a quite moment alone with Gina to find out about Charlie, but couldn't. She eventually gave up.

The evening went fast and they didn't want it to end. But Gina wanted to be alone with Charlie and Clare completely understood. They would talk some more Sunday afternoon. Gina and Charlie send their good byes

There was a phone message from Dean. He still was still trying to apologize for what he said about Jeff not wanting her anymore. He wanted her to call him, it didn't matter what hour. She felt generous all of a sudden and dialed his number.

"Dean, I'm ready to talk can you come over around nine o'clock?"

"I'll be there Clare."

"Okay bye till then."

Dean had already been up for a couple of hours before meeting Clare.

"Do you want some coffee or anything?"

"No, nothing thanks."

"Well, where do I begin? Clare, there's so much that I'm sorry for especially about Jeff. I know I had no right to demand anything, but I love you and I didn't want you to get hurt anymore."

"Wait a minute, what did you say?"

"I'm sorry for everything…"

"No" after that."

"I love you."

"No you can't, I'm not ready for this," she said getting up and walking into the kitchen puzzled by his words. She began pouring a cup of coffee. He followed her into the kitchen waiting for some kind of response, in a sad way. "I'm not trying to push you Clare or anything like that. I just wanted you to know how I felt."

"Dean, I had no idea."

"I'm sorry. It's not your fault. I just wanted more. I still do someday when you're ready."

"I don't know what's in the future for me Dean. Right now I just need friends."

"I can be that if you'll let me Clare."

"Dean all I can offer right one is friendship can you accept that."

"For right now, I'll take that."

"Then friends we are."

He placed a kiss on her cheek then back away. A few minutes later the door buzzer rang and she excused herself to answer it.

"Hello it's me." As Clare's eyes glanced toward Dean.

"Come on up."

"I'm sorry Dean but I was expecting her a little later, do you mind?"

"No, I don't can we get together Monday for lunch?" "That'll be nice."

Dean followed her to the door. Their eyes met in a guarded moment. Uneasy with the situation Clare quickly opened it and Gina was standing there.

"Good thing I came early." As her eyes glanced toward Dean.

"No it's not what you're thinking, he this is a friend and he was just leaving good bye Dean."

"See you Monday Clare, bye."

She shut the door and witnessed a big grin on Gina's face. With a raised eyebrow she asked: "Who was that?"

"Dean White I work with him."

"Anything going on between, the two of you?"

"No, Nothing."

"Couldn't tell that by him!"

"What do you mean by that?"

"The way he was looking at you."

"So we're close friends."

"Are you sleeping with him?"

"No and I don't plan to."

"You will you will."

"What am I going to do with you? Come here, and sit down."

They reminisced for the rest of the day just like old times. Clare told Gina about past events even sleeping with Chris, a secret she wouldn't even tell Jeff. She further told her about the baby she lost.

Gina understood a lot of things but that. To fall that deeply in love was the best thing possible, to betray it by sleeping with an ex boyfriend was something else. Clare admitted she was wrong, but just couldn't bring herself to tell Jeff about her night with Chris and now even if she wanted to, there may never be a chance. The way things are she might never get a chance. It seemed that no matter what she did in her life involving a relationship, it just seemed to never happen.

Gina did bring up the subject of Dean. He seemed to really care for her but for Clare there was nothing.

She broke down and cried while Gina held her in her arms consoling her, but also telling her to face facts. Jeff was gone, that relationship was gone any previous life she might have imagined was gone, but there was a man that obviously loved her and was hanging in there maybe she should give him a chance. Clare finally agreed to take it slowly with him, which satisfied Gina. Wiping her eyes and blowing her nose, Clare brought up the subject of Charlie, trying to turn the attention from her. Gina kind of squirmed when Clare brought Charlie into the conversation.

Until it hit me Gina herself was in love with him. A big grin crossed her face. She could see her eyes light up at the very mention of his name. Someone finally captured her heart. She guessed she really knew how she felt. Clare was happy things were going well for her and wished her happiness.

That evening they met up at a restaurant and to her surprise Dean was there.

"I'm sorry I'm a little late but I see you all look as if you know each other," she said. Gina knew exactly what she was thinking because she saw them getting along.

"Clare I hope you don't mind I looked in your address book and invited Dean to join us."

"No, Of course not, I'm glad you could join us Dean."

"Thanks for letting me come even though you didn't know anything about it Clare."

"Well now that we've settled things lets eat, I'm starved."

After dinner they went dancing. How Gina found the places amazed her. She always knew where all the hot spots were. Dean and she seemed to slide back into a friendship even to the point of him offering to escort her home. They said their good byes to Gina and Charlie and left.

At her apartment they stood at the door, each waiting for one to make a move.

"I had a really good time tonight Dean, thanks for coming."

"I'm glad, I wanted it to turn out well and I do apologize for you not knowing I was coming Clare."

"I think Gina had a little match making going on in her mind."

"Did it work?"

"What do you mean?" He asked as he moved closer to her.

He touched her face and kissed her. Clare responded with intensity then suddenly pulled away.

"I'm not ready for this, I'm sorry."

"Clare that's okay, take your time. I'm in no hurry."

"I have to go in I'll see you Monday Dean," she said opening the door.

Dean grabbed her arm gently. She stopped for a moment without turning. He let her go and she went inside. Tears began streaming down her face as guilt rose through her body. She felt the same as she did with Chris for a short time. She couldn't do this again to Jeff until she settled things completely.

The new work week seemed to drag by and it was made harder as she tried her best not to encounter Dean. She managed to put him off until that Friday. At that time he came to her office expecting an explanation of why she avoided him all week. She tried not to reveal what she felt for Jeff knowing he wouldn't understand. But he was being persistent and eventually Clare came out and told him.

"I can't believe you're going to him again."

"You don't understand Dean, I have to."

"Why? I thought we were getting along and maybe be more than friends."

"I can't start anything until I finish the past you have to give me this time Dean."

"What are you saying; you mean you're coming back to me?"

"I'm not promising anything at this point, but I do want to try when I get back."

"I can't believe this all this time I loved you Clare. Go, do what you have to and come back to me."

"I have to go now. I'll see you Monday morning."

With a kiss on her cheek he promptly left her office. "Clare Jeff is awake, and is staying with us at the lake please come," was the message that greeted her when she arrived home. Not believing her ears she played the message again. It was miracle. What would happen now? Overwhelmed with the news, she quickly booked a flight she ran to the bedroom to start packing. When she was done, she paced around the apartment chewing on her nails thinking about the life they could have had. She hugged herself as a smile crept on her face. Then she stared out the window without really seeing anything just empty space or at least in her mind until she heard the annoying sound of door buzzer.

"Yes can I help you?"

"Taxi."

"I'll be right down."

It was nightfall when the taxi stopped at the curb outside the airport. Clare walked in with a single thought on her mind. A grey headed gentleman sat beside her.

"Hello," he said as he settled himself.

"Are you going on business or pleasure?"

"Excuse me?"

"I'm sorry I tend to be a little nosey when I'm flying please forgive me."

"That's quit alright."

"So, which is it business or pleasure?"

"Neither."

"Oh I see you must have had a terrible fight with him."

"I'm sorry, but I'm not into discussing personal matters with strangers."

"You remind me so much of my daughter, the beauty, wit, and even spunk. I miss her terribly."

"Where is she if I may ask?"

"She died last year in a car accident."

"I'm very sorry for your loss."

Once the ice was broken Clare found herself telling a total stranger about her life. They talked as if they had known each other for years. She told him things that she hadn't even told her own mother. She needed to unload and he got the job. The kindness and the understanding he showed her made her think he must have really loved his daughter. The way he worshiped her memory was like her feelings for Chris. A feeling that even then, still knolled at her.

By the time the plane landed the peace she felt after talking to him seemed to engulf her whole being. Before disembarking, the grey hair man whose name was Dustin told Clare: "life is very short to worry about the past or even the future. It could cause missing out on the simple pleasures that are all around you."

She didn't quite understand it at first or even the small hug ending with a particular smile on his face as he left. She guessed she'd have to think about it on the drive out to Lake Merced. She picked up her small piece of luggage and proceeded to the rental car section. Once all the papers were signed she was ready to pick up the car and go. The drive would give her time to pull her thoughts together and prepare her for when she saw Jeff. The closer she got to the lake the more the nervous she became.

By the time she pulled into the driveway her heart felt as though it would jump right out of her chest. She stopped the car felling a numbness surge through her body. She rested her head on the steering wheel taking deep breaths until she managed to clam herself. I can do this she told herself.

Putting the car in gear and pressing on the gas she slowly pulled up to the house looking around when a familiar sight caught her eye. He stood at the same spot starring out across the water. Clare stopped the car and shut off the engine. She opened the car door cautiously hoping that he wouldn't hear. He didn't turn around and she proceeded toward him. The breeze off the water softly blew through her hair.

You always loved starring out across the water," she said to him.

"Yes I still find it comforting even in these times."

He turned to face her and she gasped holding her hand over her mouth, as the terror of his empty face starred right at her.

"I get that a lot these days and I can't understand why."

Clare tried to regain her composure and focus her eyes on something else other than his face.

"Do I know you? They tell me that some of my memory is gone. But other parts seem a bit fuzzy."

"That's understandable considering what you've been through."

"You didn't answer my question."

"What question was that?"

"Do I know you?"

"I guess you could say that we knew each other once."

He turned to face the water again and became silent. As he gazed out past the waves, tears rolled down Clare's face, not being able to hold them back.

"You don't have to cry. I've heard enough of that to last me a lifetime."

"I'm sorry I won't cry any more."

Still watching the water, he didn't turn to face her but she could tell he needed to say something, but was holding back.

"You know," he said "I heard what you said about knowing me, but there're things I don't remember maybe someday I will. I don't want to hurt you. If I do, I don't mean to but at this point what I really need is a friend."

"Jeff, you have plenty of people who care a great deal about you."

"I know people care but no one is my friend, I need a friend."

Tears streamed down his face as he looked into Clare's face. The look held on his face was intense enough to strike out. Seeing this Clare took his hands into hers, holding them tight.

"I'll be your friend, Jeff and if you need me I'll be there."

With those comforting words Jeff pulled Clare close into his arms, embracing her body with his. Although he seemed different the feelings Clare once knew was still there. Just as strong as it ever was, that she found herself holding Jeff just as tight as he was holding her. Losing herself in the moment, reality broke in and she pulled herself away turning toward the water.

"What's the matter did I do something wrong?"

"No Jeff it's me."

"You must forgive me I sometimes do things without realizing what other people might feel, but holding you seemed so right to me somehow but I just can't remember." "Don't worry about anything, I'm not offended in any way, but I must ask you not to hold me anymore that way."

"Why? I don't understand."

"Just trust me on this please it has to be this way."

"I don't understand you, but I'll do whatever you want me to do. Just please don't leave me."

"I won't for the time being but soon I must go."

Grabbing onto Clare's hand Jeff began walking down the path not quite sure where he was going but to Clare a much familiar path. Hesitating slightly, Clare gave in even to the point of enjoying herself a little.

The rest of the day they spent together getting to know each other again at least on Jeff's part. But Clare saw a side of Jeff she had never seen before. Almost like no pressures of life ever touched.

Evening was setting in and Clare had to go, but Jeff was convincing enough to get her to do things she normally wouldn't. He begged her to stay at his grand parent's house. Against her better judgment she agreed to stay. Jeff went upstairs to bed leaving Clare with his grandparents.

Once alone, Jeff's grandmother asked Clare to go into the kitchen for a cup of tea.

"I'm glad you stayed Clare. I've wanted to talk to you."

"You've asked a lot of me Mrs. Baines."

"Please call me Martha. I know what I've asked, but I love my grandson."

"So do I Martha, I've had my heart ripped from my chest and I'm still trying to recover from everything before you called. I decided to get on with my life without Jeff."

"I am sorry for everything you've gone through but you must understand my feelings, I just want my grandson back."

"I know how you feel some parts of Jeff I feel are still there but there is another side to him. I don't know how I am to deal with that. I can't stay forever. I have a life back in Washington; eventually I must return to it."

"I know what I'm asking. I'm getting up in years and I just want him to be secure to have someone he can depend on." "But he has parents."

"Yes but you see where he is at."

He's a broken toy to them isn't he?"

"Yes, that's why I called you besides Jeff seems to connect with you. He's just looking for someone to be his friend. Someone to accept him the way he is now."

"I don't know if I can be that for him."

"I do understand what you're saying but the love you had for him must make you want to help him."

Clare agreed to stay a little while.

"But I left some unfinished business back in DC that I have to address."

"You're going on with your life aren't you?"

"Don't you think I deserve it?"

"Yes I suppose so well, I guess I'd better get up to bed this old body is worn out. Goodnight Clare. See you in the morning."

"Good night Martha."

The rest of the night she spent thinking about what Martha had said. She knew what she was asking of her but she couldn't watch the man she loved struggling, trying to understand life. She had to think of herself and what she wanted and that was a man, a whole man. She knew that it seemed selfish, but she wanted a life and that life seemed to be in DC with Dean.

Tears streamed down her cheeks as she sobbed heavily. A hand lightly touched her shoulder.

"Why are you crying?"

"Jeff I thought you went to bed."

"I'm sorry Clare, I heard you crying and I to had to come and see."

"I'm just a little sad, that's all, because I have to leave soon."

"No Jeff I came for you.

Tears poured down Jeff's face. He knew in his heart she had to let go.

"I want you to go Clare. I have to learn by myself. I feel the connection between us. I don't understand it but this I do know, you came to me when I needed you now you have to go."

"Jeff, do you know what you're saying?"

"I'll always cherish you in my heart, this is right."

He rushed out of the room crying as a stunned Clare stood watching. What just happened before her eyes? This was the man she once fell in love with a long time ago somehow trying to emerge. Puzzled by this Clare sat down in the chair, shaking her head while running her hands through her hair. In her mind she knew he was right and it was time to go but her heart felt different. Leaving Jeff again meant probably never seeing him again ever, and Clare wasn't ready for that. But the decision was already made for her by Jeff himself and that decision must be respected no matter what feeling she had. She went to bed although she didn't expect to get much sleep.

The following morning Jeff was up bright and early with questions for his grandmother. He sat at the kitchen table sipping a cup of coffee.

"Good morning grandmother."

"What are you doing up so early?"

"I need you to answer some questions and be truthful."

"Jeff darling what do you mean? Why don't you go back to bed you look as though you didn't get much sleep last night."

"Grandmother please I love you but don't treat me like a child,

I know that I've changed after my accident, please answer my questions."

"I'm sorry my sweet Jeff. What do you want to know?" "Clare, how well did I know her, I have these feelings in me that I don't understand."

"What do you mean Jeff?"

"We were together before the accident weren't we?"

"Yes."

"I was very much in love with her wasn't I?"

"Yes, most likely you would have married."

He bent his head to the table. The gentle hand of his grandmother comforted him a little. Rising up, his grandmother proceeded to tell him everything leaving nothing out, not even the baby that they had lost.

Stunned, he got up from the table and walked over to the window and starred.

Afraid that she had revealed too much information, she turned to leave the room. In that instance, Jeff turned and said: "how can I let her go now?"

"I think you know you have to Jeff I'm sorry."

"What do I say to her grandma? Goodbye."

"Excuse me am I interrupting anything?"

"No Clare Jeff and I were just having some coffee, would you like some?"

"No thank you I just came in to tell you I'm leaving this morning and to thank you both for your hospitality."

"So you're going away?"

"Yes Jeff, I think its time."

"Then I'd like to take you to the airport."

"But how can..."

"I'll have someone else drive us, please."

"But what about the car I rented?"

"Someone will take it back later."

"Then I accept. I'll be ready to go within the hour."

Jeff stood there in a daze unable to move. Finally he turned his head towards his grandmother's with a puzzled look, he ran his fingers through his hair then walked out the kitchen door.

Wanting to find some peace Jeff walked down to the lake and stared out at the water. It always seemed to give him comfort and help him to find himself. What was his life about? Things were so mixed up. The accident wiped away everything he ever knew or thought he knew and the last link to everything was leaving.

He heard Clare's voice calling his name. Turning, he watched her as she walked towards him. Jeff smiled. "I'm ready to go Jeff."

"I guess we better go then."

"Is there something the matter you seem somewhere else?"

"Just trying to sort some things out in my mind come on lets go."

With that he began walking back to the house. Clare followed him. The ride to the airport was quiet. They were both somewhat afraid to say anything. Once they arrived at the airport Clare suggested Jeff not go in with her. But he wouldn't have it, insisting he accompanied her. After checking in they proceeded to the departure gate. She had ten minutes before boarding time. Jeff seemed anxious but didn't say anything.

"Jeff what's wrong?"

"I need you to tell me something, but I'm not quite sure."

"Jeff, tell me."

Just as he was ready to say something, she had to board Jeff looked into Clare's eyes reminding her of the days before the accident, leaving her wondering whether he would ever comeback.

"Clare I know what we meant to each other before my accident."

"How did you find out?"

"My grandmother."

"She wasn't supposed to say anything."

"She had no choice. The feelings I began to feel towards you were so strong that I had to know."

"That was back then Jeff. We have both moved on."

"I'm trying to Clare but it's so hard at times, but I do promise you this, I will get my life back."

"I believe you and hope you find some peace. That's the last call for boarding."

Jeff placed his hand on her face and leaned towards her pressing his lips on her passionately. Lost in the moment Clare responded. She felt his arms embrace her body as he pulled her closer and kissed her deeply. Realizing what she was doing she pulled away and looked at him.

"I have to go Jeff, goodbye."

"Goodbye Clare."

As she was boarding the plane Jeff thought to himself in time Clare…in time.

Clare returned to her life and to Dean although slowing down the relationship. As usual she buried herself in her work trying to avoid the closeness with him which he so desperately wanted. He tried getting Clare to talk about what was bothering her but she insisted nothing was wrong. He was glad just to have her back in his life.

For Clare she promised to give him a chance to become something in her life. But one thing she was sure of, she was not going to be intimate with him for a long time.

Clare's work became her life over the next year with the occasional distraction from Dean.

"Why don't you pour us a drink Dean, while I check my messages?"

"What would you like?"

"A white wine please."

Clare waited patiently for the answering machine to rewind while looking at Dean pouring the drinks and smiled slightly until a familiar voice sounded like thunder coming in before a storm. Could it be Jeff's grandmother's voice she heard? She listened again while Dean watched her reaction. The message said that Jeff's grandfather had passed away and Martha wanted her to know.

"Are you going Clare?"

"I'm not sure yet."

"If you want, I can go with you."

"You'd do that for me?"

"You know I would do anything for you Clare."

"Well, I guess I'll go."

"Can I ask you something without you getting upset?"

"I think I know what you're going to say, I know Jeff will be there, we settled thing long ago."

"Are you sure?"

"Yes. You don't have to worry."

She put her arms around him so her eyes would not meet with his afraid he would discover how frighten she really was. She continued to assure him that her life had grown from her past. Reluctantly agreeing with her Dean said he would make all the arrangements for the following day. With a kiss on her lips he left.

As she closed the door, Clare turned around and leaned her head against it taking a deep breath. She lingered for a moment or two as her mind wandered to the last encounter with Jeff. Breathing a bit faster she turned out the lights and headed to bed.

When the alarm sounded, she could hardly get out of bed. Dean called. He would pick her up in a couple of hours. After hanging up the phone Clare couldn't stop her mind from wondering about Jeff. How he was doing? Did he go back to work? Did he regain what he had lost? Running her fingers through her hair, Clare returned to the bedroom and got dressed.

Time seemed to get away from her. When the buzzer went off, without even answering it she unlock her door to let Dean in.

"Are you ready?"

"I'll be ready in a moment."

"Are you okay?"

"Sure. Let's just go okay."

"We don't have to do this Clare if you don't want to." "No. I'm sorry, I didn't mean anything I just, and I can't explain it."

"You don't have to say anything, let's just get in the cab and go."

"Thank you."

As Dean opened up the car door Clare touched his face and smiled. The closer the plane got to San Francisco the more frigidity she became. Finally, she leaned her head against the seat with her eyes closed.

A tear slid down Dean's face as the reality of the person he loved didn't quite feel the same way about him. He turned his head to wipe the tear away. For the rest of the flight he didn't say anything. He stared out the window until they landed in San Francisco. Just before departing the plane, Clare put her hand on his and looked into his eyes.

"Thank you for coming." Driving to the hotel, Clare thought, this town is really beautiful.

"I'd like to see some of the sights before we go home," Dean told her.

"That would be nice"

Going up the elevator to their rooms, Dean made small talk, trying to comfort Clare without much success. "Would you like to get something to eat before going out to the lake house?"

"I'm sorry, but I need to go by myself, please forgive me."

"I understand Clare. I'll be here waiting for you."

"What would I do without you?"

"I hope you never have to."

With that Clare turned and went back to the elevator. As the doors started to close she raised her hand and waved with a smile on her face.

Disappointed Dean continued to the room putting Clare's luggage in hers and then went to his. Sitting on the bed he just starred hoping that he hadn't lost her.

Clare however needed to get to the lake although maybe for the wrong reasons but she needed to see Jeff. As she drove up the driveway, there in her sights was the house she fell in love with so many years ago. Stopping the car and getting out she was greeted by Martha, thrilled to see each other after such a long time.

"I'm sorry for your loss, is there anything I can do?"

"You already have by just being here. I've missed you. Why didn't you call or write us?"

"You know why."

"He's missed you a lot. You'd be proud of him."

"He's here isn't he?"

"You'll find him down by the lake. Go see him."

As Mrs. Baines turned and went back into the house, Clare proceeded to walk down to the lake. As she drew closer she could see someone with Jeff. It was a woman and they seemed to be very friendly, Clare was almost jealous. Who could this person be and what did she mean to Jeff?

Clare, you're here."

"Hello Jeff, how are you doing?"

"I'm better now that you're here."

"I just got done speaking to your grandmother. She's holding up pretty well under the circumstances."

"Let's walk. I have a lot to tell you. That will be all for right now Jennifer. I'll see you at the funeral. If you need me call."

"I will."

She gently kissed Jeff on the cheek and then walked back towards the house."

"I'm sorry; I forgot to introduce you to Jennifer, my secretary."

Jeff watched her as she walked away then he turned and faced Clare smiling. He pointed his hand for her to walk with him side by side.

"Why didn't you keep in contact?"

"I guess I just wanted to go on with my life."

"And have you?"

"I'm working on it, but I see you have."

"What do you mean?"

"Oh yes! Jennifer. She's my secretary and my friend."

'It looked like more."

"I guess it could be. She's been there for me where no one else was."

"I'm happy for you."

"I too have someone in fact he's here with me."

"Where is he? I'd like to meet him."

"He's back at the hotel, but he'll be at the funeral tomorrow."

"I look forward to meeting him."

"Well I guess I better get back to the hotel. Dean will be waiting for me."

"Do you have to go right now? I thought we could hang out for awhile."

"I guess I could stay a little longer."

"Good, good, you know this is my place now."

"That's wonderful. You've always loved it here."

"You know Clare I know what we had before my accident. I'm

sorry I never remembered, but I have managed to pull my life back with the help of Jennifer."

"I can see that and I'm very happy for you."

"You don't understand what I'm trying to say."

"Please don't I have to go, I'll see you tomorrow."

Walking away from a bewildered Jeff, Clare went straight to her car with tears flowing down her face and drove away.

Watching out the window, Grandma Baines shook her head. Jeff watched the car drive away, walked up to the house and sat down in the kitchen. Martha came over and touched his head and told him things would work out. Jeff however didn't know how that was possible. Getting up from the table he walked into the other room, so he could be alone to think. A lot of things had happened in the past few days and putting tomorrow's funeral on top was more than he could bear.

The night seemed to fly by when the sun peaked through the bedroom window. Dragging himself out of bed, he headed for the shower as if it were a chore. The running of the water as it splashed off his face didn't seem to take the anxiety of the day away.

Clare herself didn't fare any better and she didn't hide it from Dean as she ate a quite breakfast with him. She picked at the eggs, not really eating them. Dean watched and pondered at what he was seeing. Was she upset about the funeral or who was going to be there?

"Are you alright Clare?"

"Sure. What makes you ask that?"

"Oh I don't know, you seem like you're somewhere else."

"I'm fine, I'm just thinking about today."

"Is there anything I can do?"

"No in fact I have some things to do before we go to the funeral. I would like to leave, just after to go home."

"But I thought you wanted to spend some time with Mrs. Baines."

"I did but there will be so many people around her that it would be impossible to do that."

"Whatever you say Clare."

"Excuse me Dean; I'll see you later for the funeral."

"But, Clare."

Leaving the table abruptly Clare disappeared through the doors. Instead of going to her room she walked outside and hailed a cab. As one stopped she got in and told the driver to take her to the club where she had met Jeff.

Once there she got out and walked down to the water and stood watching the waves roll to the shore. What seemed like an eternity was only moments when she heard a voice behind her.

"This was always a special place for us."

"You remember this place?"

"Bits and pieces of it."

"I'm really glad for you Jeff."

"Are you Clare?" He asked looking deeply into her eyes as if he was waiting for permission to touch her. Raising his hand to her forehead, he pulled her closer and began kissing her. Responding, Clare kissed him back joining them together even for a moment as they once were. Losing themselves in each other, thoughts of how they once were rushing through Clare's mind. She pulled away. "What are we doing? We're not the same people, too many things have changed."

"I know that things are different but we're connected, I can feel that and I think you can too."

"That may be, but I can't!"

"Clare, I love you."

"No."

Running away Clare cried profusely with one thought on her

mind, getting away from Jeff. Reaching the hotel she went straight to her room to clean up for the funeral. Once done, she knocked on Dean's door.

"Clare, where have you been, I've been so worried."

"I'm sorry Dean; I just had some things to do. We'd better get going otherwise, we'll miss the funeral."

"Clare, Clare."

"Come on Dean we'll be late," she said walking away to avoid the situation. She waited for Dean at the elevator.

Knowing not to say anything to her he joined her in silence.

Just before arriving Clare looked at Dean and saw a tear slide down his cheek.

"I'm sorry."

"Sorry about what Clare?"

"Everything I suppose."

"I don't understand Clare, what do you want?"

"I don't know. Just stop the car, I can't go."

"Clare we're almost there."

"Stop the car Dean I can't go, I want you to go for me and make my apology I'm going home."

"Home, to DC?"

"No, home to Ohio. I need some time to think about things."

"But what about us?"

"I don't know at this point if there is an us anymore."

"But, Clare."

"Please Dean; if you have any feelings for me at all you'll just do this."

"Alright Clare I will but if you need anything call me."

"I will."

She turned and walked away down the sidewalk wiping tears off her face. She stopped and hailed a cab. Instructing the driver to take her to the airport, Clare turned and looked back toward the direction of the funeral home and whispered goodbye.

Dean arrived at the funeral and sat by himself. Later on following the funeral he walked up to Mrs. Baines and gave his condolences to her in which she invited him to eat with them. Dean accepted graciously and headed back with them. As he entered his car he was interrupted by someone. "Where's Clare?"

"She couldn't make it, she sends her apologies."

He faced the man and their eyes met.

"You're Jeff aren't you?"

"Yes I am and I take it you're that other person who came from DC with her."

"Yes my name is Dean White."

"I'm glad to meet you Mr. White. Tell Clare I am sorry she couldn't be here and that I'll contact her later."

"I'm sorry but I can't do that. She caught a flight back home."

"I hope there's nothing wrong."

"No, she just had to go."

"I guess I was hoping to get to talk to her one more time."

"Don't you think you've talked enough to her, confusing her not knowing what she should do. I've waited for her along time."

"So have I."

"But you weren't always there."

"Not by choice and I assure you this is not getting us anywhere."

"I think I'll go."

"No please I'm sorry. Sometimes I don't know who I am, but I'm learning everyday how people are. Please I've waited my whole life for her."

"So have I."

"I understand were you are coming from but we have a history together."

"A history you can't even remember is what I understand."

"Some of that may be true, but what I remember is that I love her."

"You can't even take care of her," Dean said.

"Shouldn't she be the one who decides that?"

"That's exactly what she's doing and I'm confident that it will be me. Good bye," Dean said.

"What's wrong with you Jeff?"

"Nothing Mother."

"We know something is brothering you son."

"I guess it's just the day, I'll be okay."

"It's that Clare Jenkins isn't it? Ever since she showed up you became, oh I don't know."

"You don't know what your saying mom."

"You need to forget her and get on with your life."

"I have gotten on with my life. Where have you been Mother? Oh I forgot all the parties and life back in Berkley."

"Now son don't you talk to your mother that way."

"You both were against her from the start; we probably wouldn't have made it even if I didn't have the accident."

Shaking his head Jeff headed out to the lake. Not knowing what to do Grandma got up and went down to talk to him.

"They don't understand, I don't know if I even understand."

"I think you do and know what to do about it."

He turned and looked at her. She had a smile on her face with one raised eyebrow.

"Go make amends. Win her back and bring her back here to live."

"But what about Jennifer?"

"That's something that you will have to decide for your self."

"Grandma, she's been there for me when no one else has, other than you and grandpa."

"I know but in your heart do you really do love her?

"When I'm with Clare, I feel or at least I think I feel how it was before the accident."

"I guess you'll just have to search your heart, and do what you feel is right."

"I love you grandma."

"I love you too Jeff."

Back in Ohio Clare too was a making decision, hiding her feeling from her parents wasn't easy. They could sense something but never brought it up. They knew in time she would tell them.

Seeing all her old friends brought back pleasant memories of her growing up even the news of Chris being married seemed to please her. Evolving into who she was took a lot of discipline and just maybe made her look at life and not the happiness that everyone else seemed to share. Clare did finally decide to tell her mother about everything.

Not being able to sleep, she went into the kitchen to make a cup of coffee. Her mother joined her.

What's the matter Clare? I know you haven't been sleeping well won't you tell me what's wrong."

"Oh mom my life is a wreck."

"Whatever do you mean? Look at you, you're successful, beautiful?"

"I don't mean that way, I love my job and I'm good at it by my personal life needs something."

"Maybe what you need is a change."

"Yea I do and I've made a decision I'm going to transfer out of DC."

"I didn't mean to go that far."

"I know mom. But hiding from everything that's wrong isn't going to help me at this point. I just need to do something."

Leaving her mother in confusion Clare went back up to bed.

Knowing what she was going to do the next day. That night she tossed and turned until finally deciding to get up and looked out the window as she had done so many times before. She took a shower and went down stairs and made coffee.

"I see you made coffee," her mother said coming into the kitchen.

"Sit down and have a cup with me."

"You seem better this morning Clare. Did you sleep well?" "Actually no but that's okay. By the way I'm going back to DC to pack at the end of the week and then I'm coming home to stay for awhile."

"I thought you love it in DC."

"I do but I need a change. I'm going to ask for a transfer and I thought I'd stay here until it came through, if that's alright with you."

"Of course it is are you sure?"

"I think so."

"I don't understand."

"I'm sorry mom I don't mean to upset you. I'll work it out you'll see. I think I'll take a walk before breakfast."

Getting up from the table Clare walked out the kitchen door and headed toward the meadow. She could see the sun glistening on the lake in the distance. As she came closer to approaching the side of the lake she stopped. Looking at the water remembering all the times Gina and she had at Lake Merced with Jeff and his friends. Smiling to herself she thought, I'm alright with everything now. Jeff and I can go on with our lives and hold tight to the memories we once had. Holding her arms tightly around herself, Clare turned and walked back to the house.

She contacted Ambassador Craig. When he answered his phone she wasn't sure what to say. But once his calming voice started to speak, Clare felt at ease telling him what had happened and about her decision to leave DC. Ambassador Craig didn't quite agree with her decision but supported it. And now the hard part, to tell Dean. He was the one person she had put through so much, and now she was breaking up with him.

"Dean White speaking, he answered.

"Dean it's me Clare."

"I've been worried Clare but I wanted to give you some space, are you alright?"

"Yes Dean I have something to tell you and I'm not quite sure how to start."

"Just say it Clare."

"Well I know you've been there for me and I do appreciate everything but you deserve a life."

"What are you trying to say Clare?"

"I'm transferring out of DC. I'm staying with my parents until its effective."

Silence came over the phone as each of them waited for the other to speak.

"Why?" He finally broke the silence.

"I have to Dean."

"What about us Clare?"

"There is no us Dean, I'm sorry."

"I knew you should have never gone to San Francisco. we were alright until that funeral."

"No, you're wrong this has been coming for a long time. I just didn't have the courage to do anything about it until now."

"It's because of him isn't it Clare? Well I hope he makes you happy, even though I know he won't."

"Dean please understand."

Hearing the phone click in her ear, she knew she had hurt the one person in her life that was stable made her fell guilty. Guilty enough to almost call back and apologize but, she walked away from the phone wiping tears from her eyes. The last thing she wanted to do was to end their friendship in anger. Maybe eventually he would forgive her for everything.

The weeks went by with no contact from anyone but Gina until one Friday a call came in from the embassy. It was Barbra saying that her transfer had come threw. As she hung up the phone her mother came into the room. "Well it's approved," she said hugging her mother as she cried, holding on tight to her.

"When are you leaving Clare?"

"Tomorrow, if I can get a flight out."

"Are you sure you want to do this?"

"For once in my life I'm sure," she said not wanting her mother to see the fear in her eyes.

The night seemed to last forever, but the dawn did come. She climbed out of bed to the sound of the alarm clock. The warm sprinklings of the water against her body relaxed her uneasiness of the day to come. Breakfast was quiet and fast. Not many words were spoken. Not having any luggage, she was ready to go to the airport. The car ride to the airport was also a quiet one, almost a repeat of breakfast. On arriving, she announced that there was no need for either her mom or dad to accompany her inside. She would see them in a couple of days.

"Clare wait," her mother said as she walked off.

"Yes mom."

"We love you very much. Call us and let us know when you are returning, we'll be her to pick you up."

Rushing back to hug her mother Clare whispered: "I love you too, thanks.

Feeling better about things Clare continued back inside the airport to check in. As her parents drove off she turned for a moment to watch them and as she did she saw Chris.

"Clare fancy meeting you here. I've missed you."

"How have you been Chris?"

"My wife and I are visiting my family you did hear I'm married now?"

"Yea I heard. Congratulations. Oh! Also on the baby."

"Clare look I'd like to explain about that week end in DC with you."

"There's nothing to explain what happened, happened. I've move on since then."

"But I need to tell you…"

"I'm ready now Chris," he was interrupted.

"Susan, I'd like you to meet the best friend I ever had Clare Jenkins."

"It's nice to meet you Miss. Jenkins.

"Please call me Clare."

"So how long have you known my husband?"

"We went to high school together."

"Oh, I see."

"There's our ride honey, we'd better go. It's been nice seeing you Clare.

"The same here and congratulations again on your baby I hope the two of you are very happy," she said to Susan.

"Thank you Clare. It was very nice meeting you too."

Clare continued inside to check in and picked up her ticket. Then she headed for the departure gate.

After leaving the plane she caught a taxi, but didn't go to the office, instead she went to her apartment. She looked around at all the stuff she had accumulated. She made some phone calls to store some of her things until she could settle into her new place. After spending a couple of hours there getting things done she changed her clothes and headed to the office.

She went straight to Ambassador Craig's office. Barbra

greeted her as always then announced her arrival to the ambassador. Clare walked into his office and closed the door.

It's nice to see you Clare," he said.

"Ambassador I feel I must explain everything to you." "There's no need to explain Clare."

"Yes there is, you deserve to know."

She explained everything that had happened to her. He told her that he understood everything but did not agree with her choice of action.

"Clare I appreciate everything you have done for me and hope that someday I can do the same for you."

She thanked him and headed to her office hoping she would not run into Dean. She didn't and began packing up her things never once looking at her transfer papers.

A knock at her door interrupted her thoughts and when she turned around it was Dean.

"I heard you were back," he said.

"Yes I just came in to pack some things."

"So you're really leaving."

"Dean I want to say I'm sorry for everything."

"Please don't. I'm okay. I hope wherever you go you'll be happy.

"I haven't even opened the envelope yet to see where I might be."

"Well I guess I'd better let you get back to what you're doing. I'll miss you Clare. Goodbye," he said and turned and left her office closing the door behind him. Clare knew in her heart how badly she had hurt him so badly that sorry just didn't do it. She felt she should go after him but something held her back. Wiping the tears from her eyes she finished the last box. All were labeled and everything was ready to be stored until she was settled in her next job.

As she arrived at her apartment, the movers came. She showed them what needed to go in storage and having already packed her bags for the airport; she took one final walk around the town that she loved. The sights, sounds, the beauty and all the fond memories she had of this place she took in.

By the time she reached her apartment the movers were finishing up with the last of the boxes. The apartment was bare, as if she was never there. Going into the bedroom she called for a taxi, picked up her suitcases and headed to the front room, sitting her suitcases by the door. When the taxi arrived she walked out the door without looking back.

Clare smiled slightly as they pulled into the driveway of her parent's house. She told them she was tired and went upstairs to her room.

Waking up the next morning, she took a shower and then sat down at the window. In the distance near the lake she could see someone waving. The figure came slowly toward the house, until finally coming close enough in view. It was Jeff. Startled, yet excited, Clare rushed down stairs and out the door, running towards him her heart raced. As she reached him, he extended arms. They embraced, holding each other tightly.

"How did you know where I was?"

With a smile on his face, he said: "Dean told me."

"Dean?"

"Yea, I guess he knew you better than you thought."

"I'm glad you came."

"I love you Clare. I may have lost most of my memories of the past but this I know for sure; my life is nothing without you."

"Jeff, I don't know what to say."

"Clare what I'm trying to say is that I want to marry you right now and take you home with me."

"Come on, what do you say?"

"I guess my answer is yes, yes, yes," then a thought went through her head when she suddenly pulled away.

"Jeff, my transfer."

Bursting out laughing Jeff told her not to worry. "Why are you laughing at me?"

"Because you know those transfer papers, you obviously never looked at them."

"What do you mean?"

"I had a little talk with your boss; you're transferred to San Francisco."

"How did you…"

"Will you stop trying to figure it out and just kiss me?

She did and they looked at each other…hand in hand and walked over to the water and stared. For the longest time they stood there gazing out at the water.

"Do you remember the first time we met?"

"Of course I do. It was on the plane."

"I thought you were the most annoying person I'd ever met."

"And I knew at that moment that some day I'd marry you." "I guess then, you were right," she said kissing him once more.

They held each other as they turned back to staring at the water.

End